# Drylor

## Book 1:
## The First Artifact

## Ryan Tomasella

iUniverse, Inc.
Bloomington

# Drylor
## Book I: The First Artifact

*iUniverse books may be ordered through booksellers or by contacting:*

*iUniverse*
*1663 Liberty Drive*
*Bloomington, IN 47403*
*www.iuniverse.com*
*1-800-Authors (1-800-288-4677)*

*ISBN: 978-1-4502-9992-3 (sc)*
*ISBN: 978-1-4502-9993-0 (ebk)*

*Library of Congress Control Number: 2011902612*

*Printed in the United States of America*

*iUniverse rev. date: 4/26/2011*

# Chapter 1
# Amnesia

"Umph, where … where am I?" a young man asks himself.

After shaking off the initial confusion, he sits up and looks around, trying to figure out what is going on. Upon looking around, he notices that he is being carried through some sort of underground city in a cage. The tops and bottoms of the cage are made of solid wood that are held together by thick metal straps. Underneath the cage are two metal bars that are tied down with rope. They span out at least five feet in front of and in back of the cage.

The bars are in place to assist the guards who are carrying the cage through the city. On each side of the cage there are four guards, two for each bar. The man manages to catch a glimpse of himself in a window. He is about five foot seven with light, golden brown hair coming down three inches off his head. He has cobalt blue eyes, which stand out in his boyish face. He isn't wearing anything more than a few pieces of tattered cloth. Everything else he came to the city with is hanging outside of his cage in a large cloth sack.

While passing by the window, the man tries to remember his name but can't. After being hit over the back of the head by the guards, a mild case of amnesia must have came on, causing the man's head to pulsate in pain. Each time he hears a noise, it echoes through his head like a bad morning after a night of drinking. While passing one house, he spots two young kids playing with a small ball. They are bouncing it off the wall of a house, playing with each other.

Watching the kids play causes a memory to surface, fuzzy at first, but then as clear as day. Everything goes blurry as one memory becomes as clear as day. He can see himself, back when he was no older than five, playing with another young girl. He felt a connection to this girl, a very strong one. Maybe she was his sister, his cousin, or his friend. He didn't know. They were bouncing a ball off a wall just like the kids on the street. He and the girl were giggling and laughing, having a good time. He could hear words muttered from an older lady standing in a doorway yelling to them.

He felt a connection to this lady too, more of a motherly connection. She waves the kids over, and just as she is about to say his name, the vision ends. The man grabs his head before falling backward into the cage.

"Hey, you! Stay still in there!" one of the guards yells out.

The man completely ignores the guard and holds his head in the palm of his hand, trying to comprehend what he just saw. While being carried through the city, the man notices all the attention he is drawing to himself. Families are rushing out of their houses and into the streets to watch him being carried in the cage. They are all curious about what he did to get in that cage, much like he is. Without much more to do, the man leans back in his cage and watches out the front to see where he is being carried.

Right now, he is in a residential area of the town. On each side of the street, there are small homes and shops. Most of them are only one- or two-room homes, giving him the impression that this is the poor section of the city. After a few minutes of being carried through the residential area, the man comes out to a large, wide open section. There are targets at the far ends of this section, with the archers practicing their aim on them. Closer to the path that the cage is being carried along he can see men sparring with each other or with a stuffed target dummy.

Watching the men spar with each other triggers something, just like before when watching the kids play ball. But this time it imbues a strong sense of accomplishment into the man. He sees himself brawling with someone of his own race, someone older. The man he was fighting was much wiser and much stronger than him. Both of them were wearing silver armor that glistened in the sun. The armor bore the symbol of a sword and shield. He could feel other people watching him while fighting this man, but he didn't know why.

While watching this fight, he could hear the words repeated in his head, "You are now a member of the Royal Guard of Genisus." That sentence keeps echoing throughout his mind while he watches the vision. After defeating the older man, another man approached him. He was wearing a crown and being escorted by four men dressed in similar attire to him at the time. In the king's hands was a short sword. The sword was laying over top a red piece of fabric in both of the king's hands. As the king approached him, he kneeled down and held the sword up.

A sudden wave of satisfaction came over him, an overwhelming feeling of victory and accomplishment. The man reached down and grabbed the sword before holding it as high as he could into the air. The crowd around him broke into applause, whistling and making as much noise as they possibly could. After they quieted down, the king looked up and into his eyes to say, "You are now a member of the Royal Guard of Genisus."

Just like that, he is back in the gloomy underground city again. The bright, vibrant, sunny area of Genisus is gone. He looks around and notices that everyone here looks different than the people in his vision. They have darker, more bluish skin. Their ears are pointy, just like an elf, but they look nothing like the elves of Felcon to the north. While the he is still trying to understand his vision, the dark elves carrying him through the city start to speak.

"Slex hs csy xlmro xli omrg mw ksmrk xs hk xs lnq?" one dark elf says in an unknown tongue.

"Ibigyxi lmq fu qsvrmrk," the second dark elf replies with a slight chuckle.

The man has no idea what the dark elves are talking about among each other, but he knows whatever it is, it isn't good. Farther past the area where he saw the men sparring are jail cells. They must use the prisoners as live targets for them to practice against. Inside each of the jail cells sit people from all different races. There are elves, humans, half-elves, dark elves, dwarves, gnomes, and even a few halflings. While being carried past the jail cells, one of the half-elves looks up and spots the man in the cage. He rushes to front of his cell and throws his arms past the bars before beginning to shout.

While the man is shouting out of his jail cell, a dark elf guard walks up and smashes him back into his cell with his shield. "Silence, whelp!" the dark elf yells out before returning to his post. Shortly after passing the jail cells, the smell of smoke fills the air as well as an immense amount of heat. The sounds of crackling and burning wood can be heard as the cage rounds the corner and starts heading toward a large bonfire.

The man's eyes light up in fear, scared of being thrown into the bonfire and scared of another rush of memories from his past. This time he sees a town, the same town he and the young girl were playing in earlier. In the town, there are about a dozen houses with a well right in the center. The houses are clumped around the well. There are six on each side and two roads leading in and out of the village, one to the north and one to the south. Surrounding the village is a thick forest that eventually grows into a mountainside. Small brush and trees dot the forests floor. Since the village is so small, there is no doubt that everyone knows each other and almost everything about each other.

He can see the whole town visible before his eyes in perfect condition. But as he gets closer to the bonfire and can feel the heat coming off of it, flashes of the town being destroyed start to happen. The houses in his vision are burning to the ground; people's screams can be heard echoing through his head. There are dozens of bodies that fill the streets of the city.

The man brings a hand up to his face and covers his mouth, feeling sick because of the vision he is seeing. He closes his eyes and shakes his head side to side, mumbling, "No … no … no …" out loud over and over. He can't remember the people in his vision or the village that is being burned, but the emotions he has for everything are so real. When he looks up and opens his eyes, a man's face appears in front of that burning village.

The man has scarlet red hair coming down far past his waist and a face that strikingly resembles something very familiar. His eyes are jet black; looking into them almost feels like you are spiraling down into an abyss. The man's face has a small scar on his right cheek like a sharp blade just barely grazed it. Although he can't tell who this man is, he can tell he is evil. The man in this vision is evil to the core, with no chance of redemption at all.

Right as he recovers from this vision, he finds himself being carried into a palace. The steps the guards are walking on are made of pure gold, as are the statues around him. Everything is glistening in the light that the torches give off like it has just recently been polished. There are two guards stationed at every door throughout the palace. It would be impossible to escape even if given the chance.

After rounding the last corner in the palace, the guards set down the cage and open the front of it. They reach in and grab both of the man's arms, forcefully pulling him out and pushing him forward down on the red carpet beneath him. At the end of the room sits a man wearing purple robes on a throne. He has a golden crown that has just recently been polished, much like everything else around him. The crown has little red and green gemstones perfectly spaced throughout it.

The guards push the man all the way up the right carpet before striking him down to his knees before the king. When he looks up, the king stares him straight in the eyes.

"What is your name, boy?" the king asks him.

"I … I don't know …" the young man responds, feeling silly that he doesn't even know his own name.

"Your childish games will not be tolerated in this city. Tell me at once, or you will not live to see another day," the king says out loud, the frustration in his voice obvious.

"Before being brought here, I was struck on the back of the head. I do not remember my name."

"That is enough! Guards, kill him," the king says, raising his hand and beginning to stand up.

The guard to the man's right raises his sword and starts to bring it down before being interrupted. "Stop! He speaks the truth!" another voice calls out.

A younger dark elf steps out from behind the throne. He has on a long white robe with a hood covering his face.

"I can sense the man's amnesia; he truly does not remember who he is," the hooded man says out loud.

"Are you sure of this, Pelisus?" the king asks.

"I am positive, your highness."

"Very well then, take him to the jail cells until I decide what I want to do with him," the king says out loud, flicking his hand and walking away.

The guards that carried the man in grab his arms and escort him to the jail cells that they passed earlier. They push him into one of the only available jail cells and vigorously beat him before closing the cell door behind them and laughing. Instead of getting up and looking around, the man just lies there, struggling to breathe after the horrific beating. It seems like an eternity passes before a voice can be heard outside of the jail cell.

"Hey, you in there, get up immediately. We need to leave," a very familiar voice calls out.

"I said get up; we need to get out of here," the voice repeats itself.

When he finally pulls his head up off the ground, what the man sees is not what he expected. It is Pelisus, the same hooded man from inside of the throne room. The man pulls himself up to his feet. He walks over to the jail cell's bars and stares at the hooded man. Pelisus takes both of his hands and pulls off the hood, revealing his face. His skin is dark blue, much like everyone else's in this city. He has dark green eyes, much like that of vibrant grass in the spring. His hair is jet black, which blends in with his skin quite well. He has a mustache and a goatee, with very short cropped hair across the top of his head.

"I must apologize about earlier. The king is not in one of his best moods today. My name is Archmage Pelisus, and I have come to get you out of here."

"What are you talking about? What is going on?" the man asks in a very confused tone.

"You are going to be executed within the hour unless we get you out of here."

"Executed? For what? What have I done wrong?"

"You were part of a team sent from Genisus and were the only survivor left when captured," Pelisus says aloud.

"Do you know who I am?" the man asks Pelisus, hoping he has an answer.

"I am sorry, but I do not. All I know is your armor bore the royal crest of Genisus," Pelisus answers.

"Yes. I am a member of the Genisus Royal Guard, I know that much," the man says to Pelisus.

Archmage Pelisus abruptly turns to his left and watches two guards as they approach him and the jail cell. Both of the guards are talking to each other in an unknown tongue, which Pelisus seems to understand.

"Come now, give me your hand, we must get out of here," Pelisus says out loud before throwing his arm into the jail cell.

"What do you—" the man starts to say but is interrupted.

"No time for this! Give me your hand. We must go now!" Pelisus yells out loud.

The man hesitates for a few seconds before placing his hand into Pelisus's, knowing that he has no other choice. Little white balls start to appear out of the ground beneath them. A commotion arises from the guards who are walking toward Pelisus as everything starts to fade. A loud noise rings out throughout the area, followed by a bright flash of white. The next thing the man sees is trees—lots and lots of trees. While looking around, he notices that he is in a forest. There is a damp, thick mist over the forest, making it hard to see, but in the distance he is able to see a set of torches and what looks like a gate leading into a city.

Pelisus places his hand on the man's shoulder and says out loud, "We need to get moving. They will be looking for us soon."

"Lead the way," he says.

Pelisus nods before leading the man west through the woods at a hastened pace. It is difficult for the man to keep track of Pelisus and watch where he is going. With how thick the fog is in the woods, it is impossible to see any more than a few feet in front of him. Not even the light of the full moon is helping them navigate through the forest. Almost thirty minutes go by without Pelisus or the man speaking a word to each other.

They can hear the grunts and groans of the wildlife around them and the popping and cracking of the sticks beneath their feet. As time goes on, their endurance starts to fade. All of the jogging and jumping over logs is starting to take its toll on them.

"Stop," Pelisus says, stopping dead in his tracks.

Pelisus brings both hands up to his head and places his first two fingers lightly over top of his temple while his thumbs are gently placed under his chin. Pelisus starts to lightly hum as his eyes move rapidly underneath his closed eyelids.

"They are having trouble following us with the thick fog tonight," Pelisus says.

Pelisus removes his fingers from his temple and swings his hands around in the air slowly. A few seconds later, he thrusts his elbows down to his side forcefully before finally opening his eyes.

"I just erased our trail through the woods. Let's continue a little farther west just in case."

The man nods, following Pelisus through the woods again. This time they take a much more relaxed pace, moving at about half the speed as before. Both of the men struggle to catch their breath from the long jog before. About a mile farther west from the first stop, Pelisus stops again.

"This should be far enough. It would take anyone following us days to find a sign of our passing. We should make camp here. Help me collect some wood for a fire."

The man nods to Pelisus while collecting any logs and sticks he sees in the immediate area. The two of them collect wood for close to ten minutes before meeting back at the pile of sticks they've now formed.

"We should have enough to get through the night," Pelisus says to the man.

"Now how are we going to …" the man says before watching Pelisus closely.

Just like before, Pelisus closes his eyes and waves both of his hands around in the air. He takes in a deep breath afterward, thrusting both of his hands down toward the pile of sticks they collected. Almost immediately,the pile bursts into flames. The spontaneous combustion scares the man and causes him to jump backward, as he was not expecting it at all.

"It is okay, lad. I take it as you aren't around magic much?" Pelisus asks the young man.

"Um, no, not really. Well, I may have been. If I was, I cannot remember," the younger man replies. "Where are we?"

"We are in the Misty Woods, a few miles west of Terrova, the dark elf capital."

"Where is Genisus?"

"Wow, you really don't remember much, do you? Genisus is far to the north, over the great Land Bridge."

"How long will it take us to get to Genisus?"

"It would take almost a week walking, a few days on horseback."

The younger man nods to Pelisus while looking around at the woods around them. They are surrounded by dozens of different sounds. Each of them is intriguing in its own way. While looking around the camp, occasionally the younger man sees a pair of beady eyes staring at him. None of what he sees worries him because Pelisus is so close by.

"Pelisus, can I ask you something?" the younger man says.

Pelisus doesn't speak but nods instead.

"Why did you save me?" the younger man asks sincerely.

"When I was a young boy, Arknon, the king of Terrova, executed my family. He never said why, and after twenty years of reading the king's mind, I don't even think he knows why. The old prophecy of dark elves says that a young man, a half-elf, will come and abolish us from a wretched king. I've never felt so certain before in my life … I think you are that man," Pelisus says.

"Wow … That's a lot of responsibility that you're bestowing onto me," the young man says.

"We shouldn't worry about that now. You should put your head down and get some rest. You will need it for tomorrow," Pelisus adds.

The young man nods to Pelisus while lying down on the ground. With the roaring campfire so close to him, he is forced to constantly switch sides to prevent being burned. While trying to fall asleep, he occasionally opens his eyes to glance at Pelisus and see what he is doing. Pelisus just continues to sit there, staring off into the cloudless night sky. He shows no signs of being tired or any intention of going to sleep for the night. Knowing this makes the young man feel even more comfortable.

The following morning when the man awakes, Pelisus is gone. A lot of the fog from the night before has settled in the woods, and everything is a lot more calm and quiet. He sits up and looks all around the surrounding woods for Pelisus, but he is nowhere to be seen. Feeling a strong sense of betrayal, he stands up and kicks dirt on the remaining embers still burning in the fire. With the fire now completely out, he lets out a long, drawn-out sigh before continuing west again. While he is walking west, he can't help but wonder why Pelisus left him.

Why would someone essentially banish himself from his own city and then abandon what he tried so hard to save? It just makes no sense. After walking for about ten minutes, he stops to take a quick break at a nearby stream. While he is taking a sip of water, a strong feeling of being watched crosses over him. He leans up and looks around nonchalantly, acting as if he has no idea he is being watched. As he leans down to take another sip, he can feel someone sneaking up behind him. He hesitates for a moment before jumping up and spinning around to see who it is.

"Whoa, it is just me. No reason to be alarmed," Pelisus says while holding out his hand.

"I thought you had abandoned me ..." the man says to Pelisus.

"No, I was just scouting the area ahead."

"I see. Is it safe ahead?"

"Yes, but I think we should take a quick detour. You need a weapon, and I know of a nearby cave that is said to have a legendary sword that the dark elf Lun'er used."

"Lun'er? Wasn't he evil?"

"I guess that depends on who you ask. If it wasn't for Lun'er, dark elves wouldn't exist. Lun'er may have done some questionable things, but I believe that his heart was good."

"Will I, a nondark elf, be able to wield this weapon?"

"You are a half-elf, from what I can see. This means you have some elvish blood. Wielding the weapon should be of no problem for you."

"All right, then, let's go," the young man says to Pelisus while waiting for him to lead the way.

Pelisus nods and lightly smirks before pulling the hood of his robe over top his head and continuing west. Both men are quiet as they continue their journey through the woods. Pelisus stares at the ground as he walks through the woods, not paying much attention to anything around him, whereas the younger man admires the beauty of the forest surrounding them. He notices that a few of the trees stand out among the others in a very ominous way. Some of them look almost like they have faces and give the strange impression that they are watching the two men as they travel through the forest.

While walking through the woods, the man keeps an eye on the different trees he comes across. The first thing he notices is that some of the trees have slightly lighter bark then the others. The trees with the lighter bark are also softer than the other trees. When touching them, it feels like you're running your hand down rough skin rather than tough bark. While continuing through the woods, he also notices that the trees with the slightly lighter bark seem to make weird cracking and popping noises, almost as if their roots are moving beneath the ground they're walking on.

Now that the man notices all of the differences between the trees, he starts to become very curious of them. He wonders why some of the threes are so different from the rest.

"Hey, Pelisus, why are some of these trees different than the others?" the young man asks.

"Not all of them are trees. Some are Treants," Pelisus answers.

"What is a Treant?"

"A Treant is an ancient tree that has been imbued with the power of magic, which in turn causes it to come alive."

"Should we be worried about them?"

"No. Treants only harm people they find threatening. If they haven't harmed you yet, then you have nothing to worry about." Pelisus adds, "Treants usually don't harm anyone with Druidic abilities."

"What are you saying, I am a druid?" the man asks Pelisus curiously.

"This I am not sure of. I sense some form of magic in you, but I can't fully understand it," Pelisus says.

"I see … This whole memory loss thing is a bummer," the young man says.

Pelisus faintly chuckles as the conversation comes to a close. The young man and Pelisus continue their journey through the woods until about midday, at which point they finally reach the cave that Pelisus spoke of. The entrance to the cave is covered by a few fallen trees and thousands of vines that found their way through the rocks over the years. With all the delicate flowers and shrubs growing around the cave, you could tell that no one has been here for many years.

Pelisus leads the younger man up to the cave, holding any branches for him as he passes. When they reach the entrance, both men stare down at the small crack they have to enter. The crack is no more than three feet wide and seven feet high. The sides of the rock throughout the crack are rugged and rough, meaning it will be very easy to get cut while traveling through. Pelisus pulls the hood off of his head and nods to the young man before starting through the crack.

Both of the men have their backs to the wall as they shimmy through what little space they have. As they get farther into the cave, the light from the outside becomes more and more faint until eventually nothing but darkness surrounds them. After walking through the darkness for somewhere around five minutes, Pelisus hits a solid stone wall with his left shoulder. Pelisus brings both of his hands up to the sides of his head while taking in a deep breath. In between both men, a small ball rises up from the ground that is emitting a large glowing white light.

As the ball rises in the air, it lights up the whole area around them. The young man's eyes swell in excitement as he watches the ball hover around the small tunnel they're in. When Pelisus brings the ball back toward him, it lights up the area right in front of the two of them. In front of Pelisus is a large wooden rope ladder leading far up into the cave. The steps of the ladder are made of wood, while the rope is made of living vines that are growing off the wall.

Pelisus grabs a hold of the vines connected to the ladder before giving it a small tug to make sure it is steady. He nods to the younger man before climbing up the ladder. Once Pelisus is out of the way, the young man follows him. The small light ball that Pelisus is using for light is hovering between both of the men as they climb up the ladder. At the top of the ladder, there is an extremely large room. Neither of the men is able to see anything in the room but the sound of water flowing violently can be heard.

Pelisus smirks as they enter the room, bringing his hands back up to his head. When he does this, the light ball disperses in the air. This time when Pelisus exhales, dozens of torches light up in the room, one after another. When they're all lit up, both men are able to get a clear visual of the room in its entirety. The room is almost thirty feet tall and one hundred yards long. They are standing on a solid stone platform that sits right next to an underground river. The river is no more than twenty feet wide, but with how strong the current is, it would be impossible to pass.

On the other side of the room there is a small pedestal. Sitting on top of the pedestal is the sword they've come so far to get.

"The only way over there is to cross the river," Pelisus yells over the noise of the rushing water.

"But how?" the young man asks.

Pelisus kneels to the ground, bringing both hands up to his forehead. He starts to take deep breaths in and out as the other man watches curiously. A few seconds go by, and the cave starts to shake just a bit. The young man looks around frantically before spotting a large, flat rock coming out of the water. The rock is the size of a small dinner table and looks like it weighs close to eight hundred pounds. Pelisus struggles to pull it out of the water. He manages to hold it just over top of the river, yelling for the half-elf to go across.

The young man nods to Pelisus while running over to the rock and lightly stepping up onto it. With the extra weight of the young man, Pelisus grunts and groans while trying to hold the rock steady.

The rock slowly moves across the river as the young man quivers in fear of Pelisus not being able to hold the weight. Each wave from the river below smacks against the bottom of the rock and ever so slightly tilts it from one side to another.

When the man gets close enough to the other side, he jumps off the rock and rolls across the floor. Immediately after the man leaves the rock, Pelisus breaks his connection with it and stands up. Pelisus mumbles something and points to his feet before nonchalantly walking toward the river. As he steps over top the river, small white circles of light glow beneath his feet. This keeps him perfectly level with the solid ground and stops him from falling into the river below. The younger man arches an eyebrow as he watches Pelisus walk across the river without even getting wet.

Once across the river, Pelisus smirks to the man before leading him over to the pedestal with the sword. Both of the men are amazed by the beauty of the sword. It is still in perfect condition after all of these years. At the top of the sword by the blade there is a dark blue sapphire gleaming in the light of the torches. Just the sapphire alone has to be worth a few thousand gold coins. Running down the blade in the central part of the sword is a small blue line. It almost perfectly resembles the river that is behind them in the cave.

When looking closely at the line on the sword, you are able to see the small flowing river. The blue line runs all the way down the sword and into the hilt, where it stops. The sword's hilt is made of solid metal, with a picture of a water serpent engraved onto it. Around the grip of a sword is tightly wound leather with a small engraving on it. The engraving reads:

*Use this sword well, Lun'er*

The man smiles after looking over the sword and reaches down to grab it. The second he touches the sword, the cave starts to shake, and the river behind them becomes even more violent. The man's grip locks around the sword as the cave continues to shake violently. The river behind them starts to spout water all over the room as a large water serpent arises out of it. The man squeezes the handle of the sword as tight as he can as memories surge back into his mind. The surge of memories is so violent and overwhelming that he passes out.

✦ ✦ ✦ ✦

*"Von, are you okay? Von, are you there?"*

Is that … Is that my name?

*"Daddy, are you okay? Mommy, what's wrong with Daddy?"*

I have … kids? I am married?

*"I don't know, dear; just go to your room. I'll let you know when he is awake …"*

*"Von, just go! You can't save both of us …"*

I'm … I'm sorry …

*"Von, you are now a member of the Royal Guard of Genisus. Do our city proud and protect it from your brother."*

My brother? What are you talking about?

*"Von, it's your brother. He has returned!"*

What do you mean he has retur…

*Von can see the same image from before with the burning city. Everyone screaming in terror as they're all burned alive. At the end of the same vision, Von can see the man's face again, the man with scarlet red hair and jet black eyes. A smile comes across this man's face as he begins to laugh.*

*"Hey, brother …"* the man in his vision says with a slight chuckle in his voice.

"Scarlet …" Von mumbles out loud.

*"You miss me? 'Cause I'm back … and I'm coming for you, li'l bro."*

✦ ✦ ✦ ✦

Von gasps for air as he jolts back into reality. When he looks over, he can see Pelisus shouting at him, but he is unable to hear him. Von looks around the room and sees that the cave is collapsing around them. Large chunks of rock are falling off the ceiling, and water is bursting through the cracks. Von's hearing starts to come back as he looks down at his right hand. The sword from the pedestal sits in it, the hilt almost perfectly fitting the shape of his hand.

"Come on, we need to go!" Pelisus is shouting out loud at Von.

"Von …" Von mumbles out loud.

"What?" Pelisus asks, unsure of what he means.

"It's my name."

"You remember?"

"Yes."

Von grips the sword tightly and stands up. When he turns around to face the river, there is a large water serpent looking straight into his eyes. The water serpent's face is the size of a lion's. The whole body is lean and slick all the way down, highly resembling that of an eel. Coming off both sides of the water serpent are large wings, probably not used for flying but more for faster swimming. The tail of the beast is not only long but also filled with thousands of little spikes. One hit from that tail without any armor would most certainly be the last.

The face of the creature is long and almost like that of a bird. Its nose sticks out like a beak, and along the side of his face it has two large gills, used for breathing underwater.

"You have summoned me, mortal. If you wish to leave this cave alive with that sword, you must defeat me."

"Heh," Von says with a slight chuckle. "Bring it."

The water serpent lets out an ungodly loud shriek and thrusts his tail at Von. Von runs to a nearby wall and runs up it before flipping backward off it. While he is airborne, he cuts the serpent's tail with the newly acquired sword, causing dark blue blood to ooze out from the wound. When he lands, the serpent extracts his tail back to the water and pauses.

"A better fighter then I expected. This should be fun."

With another shriek, the serpent summons multiple small water serpents at Von. Von smirks and runs forward at the serpents. Pelisus launches a lightning bolt at the large water serpent while Von deals with the smaller ones. Caught off guard by Pelisus' attack, the serpent stumbles backward, smacking its head on a large rock that was falling from above. Von finishes off the little water serpents and continues toward the large one.

At the edge of the river, Von jumps and propels himself onto the serpent's body. He uses his sword almost like an ice pick as he climbs up the beast's slick, slippery body. As Von is climbing the beast it tries to attack him with its beaklike mouth. Von does the best he can to fend it off with his feet while trying to get up the beast's body. It doesn't take long for the water serpent to get lucky and get a hold of

Von's foot. The beast has his foot in its mouth, and it clenches down hard and rips Von off of its body. It swings Von around in the air before tossing him at a nearby wall. Von spins around in midair and kicks off the wall back at the serpent.

He propels himself face first at the serpent with his sword swinging in the air. The water serpent raises its tail and thrusts it forward at Von. Noticing that Von can't defend against this attack, Pelisus raises his hands and conjures a strong gust of wind to knock the beast's tail out of the way. With the tail now out of Von's path, he lands back on the serpent and swings his sword violently at the beast's head. The blade is just barely able to graze the side of the beast's face as it struggles to get Von off again.

The beast shrieks before jumping up in the air and diving head first into the river below. Von grabs on to the beast the best he can and prepares to get wet. The second Pelisus sees what the beast is doing, he casts a spell on Von, giving him gills along the side of his abdomen and also fins as feet. Underwater the beast travels through dozens of different tunnels and canals, thrusting its body into the walls to try and shake Von.

With the spell Pelisus cast on him, Von is able to safely breathe underwater and fight just as well as on land. He rips his sword out from the beast and stabs it back in, starting to climb the beast's back. Right after Von thrusts the sword back into the beast, it enters a large underwater room and kicks Von off its body into a nearby wall. Von catches himself and treads water while the beast gets ready.

"You're on home turf now. Show me what you got," Von says sarcastically.

The beast doesn't take kindly to his sarcasm and launches himself like a torpedo right at Von. Von waits until the last minute before flipping his body over the beast and thrusting his sword into the back of its neck. The beast shrieks in pain as it crashes into a wall on the far side of the tunnel. Von throws his legs over the beast and sits down on top of it before vigorously attacking the back of its neck with his sword.

The beast's shrieks of anguish are all that can be heard in the underwater tunnel. With Von still sitting on the beast's back, it raises its body up to slam itself into the ceiling. Von sees it coming, though, and spins himself around the beast to the bottom. As the beast crashes into the ceiling, Von slams his sword as deep into the creature as it can go. The sword's blade penetrates deep inside, just inches away from the serpent's heart.

The water serpent goes berserk, knowing that the end is near. It starts to swim wildly around the underwater cave, using its tail to hit all the walls, causing everything to collapse. Von tries to hold on, but he can't with how fast the beast is going. As Von spirals off of the beast's body, he smacks against one of the rocks that is sinking down to the pit below. Just as he is able to look up and see the beast, he is forced to duck again in order to avoid its tail.

He watches the beast as it swims around the room one more time. This time, Von's ready. When the beast comes around the cave this time, Von grabs a hold of a piece of its wing. Grabbing a hold of this, he pulls himself forward and thrusts his blade right into the beast's heart. Von delivers the killing blow as he lets go and pulls the sword out from the beast. The beast flails around, even more wild than before, as its blue blood fills the water around the two of them. Von turns away from the beast and starts to swim back through the tunnels they once came.

Von knows that if he doesn't get out now, he will suffer the same fate as the beast. Swimming through the tunnels, Von is forced to dodge dozens of rocks that are sinking to the abyss below. When he finally reaches the river where Pelisus is waiting for him, he leaps out and back onto land. Pelisus quickly removes his enchantment so Von doesn't suffocate on land.

"Let's go, we need to get out of here. Grab my hand!" Pelisus yells out to Von while throwing his hand at him.

Von reaches up and grabs Pelisus's hand while trying to catch his breath. Pelisus starts to channel the same spell he used in Terrova at the jail cells. In a blink of an eye, Pelisus and Von are back outside of the cave, safe and sound.

"Whoa, that was a close one," Pelisus says.

"Yeah, it was," Von replies.

Von pulls himself up to his feet and takes a look at his new sword. The sapphire is gleaming in the light that manages to find its way through the trees. Von and Pelisus take a few minutes to catch their breath and let the adrenaline in their system fade. Once they both have calmed down, Pelisus stands up and looks down to Von.

"We should probably get a move on. We may be able to reach the Western Desert by sundown if we move quick enough," Pelisus says.

Von nods to Pelisus before motioning for him to lead the way. Pelisus takes the lead and continues north through the forest. The ground beneath them is lightly trembling as the cave they got the sword from finishes collapsing. Both of them smirk from feeling the ground tremble, knowing that they were the primary cause of it and that they both came out victorious. Pelisus and Von are now venturing north through the Misty Woods on their way to the Western Desert.

While they travel further north, the changes in the landscape start to become more noticeable. The amount of trees starts to thin out, as does the amount of fog. All the forestlike shrubbery starts to change to desert-like shrubbery. The previously extremely flat landscape starts to arch and form into hills as they get closer to the hill pass that connects the Misty Woods to the Western Desert.

"So, you got your memory back?" Pelisus asks Von.

"Yeah, I got it back," Von replies.

"Well then, tell me a bit about yourself," Pelisus says.

"Uhm, well, I know my full name is Sir Von Lockfur of the Genisus Royal Guard. I remember having two children and a wife, but I can't remember their names. I also have a brother whose name is Scarlet. Well, at least I think he is my brother. I saw him in a vision of a village burning—my village. He was laughing as everyone was burning alive. At the end of the vision, he said he was coming for me …" Von says to Pelisus.

"Coming for you? What do you mean?" Pelisus asks.

"I'm not sure. I don't even fully remember who he is. I guess I haven't gotten all of my memory back yet," Von replies.

"You could be blocking a lot of it out. You don't want to remember who he is because he is a horrible person," Pelisus says to Von.

"Yeah, I guess that is always a possibility," Von replies. "So, Pelisus, I've been meaning to ask you …"

"Hush! I hear something. Get down," Pelisus says, cutting Von off.

Both of the men crouch down and listen. While Von listens to what appears to be nothing, Pelisus brings both hands up to his head and starts to channel a spell. About thirty seconds later, he breaks his channel and grabs Von's arm. Pelisus pulls Von over to two nearby rocks and ducks behind them.

"Stay quiet. I am going to channel a spell to remove our scent from the air," Pelisus says to Von.

Von stays behind the rock as motionless and quiet as can be. In the very far distance, Von can hear dogs barking. It didn't sound like a normal dog either; the bark sounded much more demonic and frightening. Minutes pass, and the sound of the bark grows closer and closer. As the sound grows closer, the single demonic bark turns into two and then three. In the tree line to the south, Von can see two dark elves emerge with a pack of dogs in front of them.

The dogs have their noses to the ground, sniffing vigorously for a scent of the escaped prisoner, Von, and the betraying Archmage, Pelisus. As the dogs grow closer to Von, his heart starts to race. Just the thought of going back to Terrova is unfathomable. The pack of dogs stops in a dry patch about twenty feet in front of the rocks Pelisus and Von are hiding behind. They sniff around the area for close to thirty seconds while waiting for their handlers to arrive.

Pelisus's spell seems to be working; the dogs are unable to follow the scent from that point. Von peeks out from behind the rock to get a good look at the dark elves' dogs. The dogs look like they were originally of the Rottweiler breed. They're fully black with brown across their faces and down by their paws. Each of the dogs has roughly six tentacle-like things hanging from the bottom of their mouths. Each tentacle was no more than six inches in length. The tentacles weren't covered in fur but instead were pinkish in color.

What purpose the tentacle-like objects serve is in no way shown. Once the dark elvish handlers reach the dogs, they look around the area for the reason they lost the scent. Von ducks behind the rock again as the dark elves look around for any clues to where they could have gone. He grips his sword tight as he hears one of the dark elves start to walk his way.

"No … If we kill these two, they will send more out of suspicion," Pelisus whispers to Von.

Von nods to Pelisus as the dark elves scout the area. The two handlers walk around the perimeter while the demon dogs are still trying to pick up the scent. The longest five minutes of Von's life is pass as the dark elves search the area. Just as Von thinks they are about to leave, one of the dogs barks. This sends shivers down both Von's and Pelisus's spines. They thought they are captured again. The dog continues to bark until one of the dark elf handlers yells at it and whips it with a leather whip. The dog yelps and growls at its handler.

"Xlic'ir ksri. Pix'w ks fego," one dark elf says to the other in a language Von cannot understand.

"They're leaving," Pelisus whispers to Von, having understood what they said.

Von nods as he listens closely to the sounds of the dark elves leaving with their dogs. It takes a few minutes until the dark elves are finally out of sight and can no longer be heard. Von tries to come out from behind the rock, but Pelisus forcefully pulls him back down.

"Wait. They're still watching," Pelisus whispers to Von.

Pelisus closes his eyes and again puts his hands up to his head, leaving Von alone to fight the boredom of waiting. Waiting for the coast to clear, Von begins to play with the sandy ground next to him. He spins his finger around in the dirt and draws crude pictures of whatever comes to mind. Close to thirty minutes after the dark elves leave, Pelisus breaks from his trance.

"The coast is clear," Pelisus says to Von.

"Yeah, I figured that out close to thirty minutes ago," Von replies sarcastically.

"We should get moving. We'll make camp up in the hill pass," Pelisus says to Von.

Von nods to Pelisus before standing up and following him further north toward the Hill Pass. The Hill Pass is a small pass between two very large hills that leads to the Western Desert. It is most commonly used by the gnolls as a trade route to Terrova and Thundon. As Von and Pelisus continue north, the changes to the scenery become much more obvious. The plant life completely changes and in some parts ceases to exist. The dry heat from the desert to the north can be felt in the air, sucking the moisture right out of it. This causes Von and Pelisus to sweat profusely.

When Von and Pelisus finally reach the Hill Pass, the sun is almost fully set in the sky. Looking at the sun over the desert, you can see silhouettes of cacti, bushes, and mountains in the distance. There is still a slight haze over top of everything as the burning heat from the desert floor is still trying to escape. Von stares off into the distance at the setting sun. Pelisus runs around frantically to collect firewood for the night.

Just as the sun completely sets, Pelisus finishes collecting wood and ignites it all into flames. With the campfire now going, Von climbs down off of a rock and walks over to the fire. He sits down next to Pelisus and looks up at the stars.

"It's beautiful out tonight," Von says to Pelisus.

"Yeah … This is the first night in a long time that I've been under the stars," Pelisus replies.

A faint smile comes across Von's face as a tear rolls down his cheek. Von puts his head down and slightly chuckles before Pelisus notices.

"What's wrong?" Pelisus asks.

"I … I'm not sure," Von replies. "Out of nowhere I just got this strong feeling of separation from someone but I don't know who …" Von says.

Pelisus nods before looking at the ground and back to the sky. There is a full moon tonight. The light it is giving off lit up the area all around Pelisus and Von, even more so then their campfire. Pelisus is able to see the pain in Von from missing whatever it is he is missing. But all Pelisus is able to do is sit there and watch the man in anguish.

"We should probably get some sleep. We have a very long journey ahead of us tomorrow," Pelisus says to Von.

Von nods to Pelisus before lying down and resting his head across his arm. The tears are still rolling down Von's face as he stares at the campfire. Luckily, the campfire muffles most of the sniveling that Von is doing, even though Pelisus already knows it is still embarrassing to him.

"I don't know what hurts more—not knowing what I miss so much … or missing it so much …" Von mumbles to himself before closing his eyes and falling asleep.

# Chapter 2
# Captured!

Von awakes the following morning by a gnoll forcefully pulling him up off the ground. The second Von feels the hand on his arm, he reaches for his sword, but the gnolls moved it beforehand. Von tries to shout out to Pelisus, but before he can, a hand is thrown over his mouth. Von throws his head back to try and hit whatever has ahold of him, but he is unsuccessful. His attempt to escape just angers the gnoll more, causing him to squeeze tighter and growl into Von's ear.

At first glance, Von notices over ten gnolls at the camp. Three of them are standing over Pelisus, who is still sound asleep. The other gnolls are busy examining Von's sword, celebrating over how much it will sell for back in Cathunder, the gnoll capital. When Von turns back to look at Pelisus, he is given a second to examine the creatures. The gnolls are very primitive creatures.

They are no taller four feet, and they share a striking resemblance to a dog. They have dark brown hair that covers the majority of their body and an indented nose. Their ears are arched in a pyramid coming off the top of their head, almost like that of a bat. When it comes to wearing armor, gnolls have to have it custom made since no other races' armor will fit them. This results in many of the gnolls just wearing loin cloths to cover up their important private areas. Also, in order for gnolls to run and stand up without falling, they are forced to use their two front paws to balance themselves.

After studying the gnolls, Von notices one of them has drawn its sword and has it risen over the top of Pelisus's body. When Von sees this, he kicks and struggles as much as he can, trying to break free or wake Pelisus up.

With one strong thrust backward, Von manages to remove the hand from his throat and slam the back of his head into the gnoll's nose. Once free, Von stumbles forward and screams at the top of his lungs, "Pelisus!"

Pelisus jolts up from sleeping and sticks his arms out to his side, sending shockwaves of force out in both directions. All the gnolls standing around him are knocked a few feet away and onto their backs. Von dashes forward and tackles the gnoll that is holding his sword. As the gnoll hits the ground, the sword is knocked out of its hand and slides across the sand. Von punches the gnoll in the face once before jumping off the top of the gnoll and over to his sword.

Now that Von has his sword, he charges head first into the gnolls, swinging it wildly. The first gnoll he comes into contact with gets a large slice across the chest, at least two inches deep. After slicing open the first gnoll, Von spins around and decapitates the second. A third gnoll rushes toward Von but is quickly finished off by a powerful thrust to the chest. Von's blade pierces through the beast's heart and out the other end of its body, causing blood to spray all over the sand.

Pelisus quickly finishes off any of the gnolls around him with a few quick and efficient fireballs. The fireballs cause the beast's fur to immediately ignite into flames. This causes a slow and painful death. After Von and Pelisus finish killing all the gnolls that attacked them, they take a look around and notice they brought a supply wagon with them. It is parked farther down the Hill Pass, to the north. They must have left it far away so they could sneak up without anyone hearing them.

The supply wagon is very poorly crafted; it is just a few pieces of wood and two wheels. Without there being any horses around to pull the wagon, it looks like the gnolls pulled it themselves. Von and Pelisus run over to the supply wagon and look around first, to see if there are any other gnolls. Once the coast looks clear, they start to rummage through the supplies to see if the gnolls have anything they can use. The first thing Von pulls out is a set of damaged leather armor that is made to fit an elf. While Pelisus is still going through the cart, Von puts on the armor. It is a loose fit, but it will work for the time being.

Von's main concern is the large sword hole through the chest area of the armor. A few of the studs that hold the armor together are also falling off. You can tell it has seen heavy use. Pelisus pulls out three emptied canteens and tosses them over to Von.

"Great, now we just need to find where to fill them up!" Von says out loud to Pelisus.

The only other thing Von and Pelisus are able to find useful in the wagon is a large burlap sack. It must have been used to carry supplies by the gnolls. The two of them check the whole wagon at least two more times before deciding to continue their journey north into the desert. Von takes a quick second before following Pelisus to admire his surroundings. To the north, there is a barren wasteland with almost no shrubbery to be seen for miles. There are large sand dunes and sand that will consistently be blowing in your eyes the duration of the time you're there.

To the south you have the Hill Pass. These are the hills that separate the Misty Woods and the Western Desert. The hills are still lush with plant life and actually have solid dirt and rocks for you to walk across. Of course, walking over the rocks would be much more dangerous, especially with all the rattlesnakes that like to hide in them. At the bottom of the hill pass to the north the wildlife just abruptly ends. Without any previous warning, you just simply stop seeing plants grow. This confuses Von. Maybe he was just thinking too much into it.

After getting a good look at all of his surroundings, Von catches back up to Pelisus. Already in a short period of time, Von is able to see how hard of a walk this is going to be. Not only is the hot sand burning his unprotected skin, but with each step, his foot sinks down into the sand. With Von having to walk like he is in the snow, accompanied with the grueling heat, it is almost unbearable. And it's only the morning.

As the day wears on, the heat only becomes worse. The sun is beating down on Von and Pelisus as they walk through the Western Desert. Von and Pelisus strip most of their clothing off, aside from a piece they wrap around their heads, and put into the large burlap sack from the supply wagon. The piece on their heads acts like a sun visor, keeping the sun out of their eyes, and also prevents their hair from being cooked in the heat. The two of them take turns dragging the sack along, but neither of them ever spend more than five minutes with it in their hands. While walking through the desert, Von spots something in the distance.

"Did you see that?" Von says, pointing in that direction.

"There is nothing out here. You're probably hallucinating," Pelisus says to Von.

Von nods to Pelisus, figuring that he is right. As they are walking, Von keeps an eye on everything around him. He watches all of the hills around the area like a hawk, waiting to see the same figure he saw before. Without seeing anything for close to thirty minutes, Von lets his guard down. Just as his guard is dropped, he hears a loud screech in the distance.

"Now you can't tell me that was just a hallucination," Von says to Pelisus.

"No. That was a lizard man," Pelisus replies.

"A what?" Von asks.

"A lizard man. They live in these parts. It usually means there is an oasis nearby," Pelisus adds.

Von turns around to look behind him. Right as he does, a large green lizard pops out of the sand below him and uses its tail to smack him across the face. Von stumbles backward and falls to the ground from the attack. He quickly shakes his head side to side, trying to shake off the attack before picking himself up. Von reaches into the large burlap sack for his sword, bracing himself for another attack.

"Von, they won't show themselves. By nature they like to play tricks on people," Pelisus says to Von.

Von squeezes his sword tightly as he waits for another attack, ignoring what Pelisus said. Before Pelisus is able to say anything to stop Von again, a strong gust blows across the desert. Von and Pelisus both are forced to cover their eyes to prevent sand from getting into them. The winds get stronger as Von and Pelisus both stumble across the sand.

"What's going on?" Von shouts out to Pelisus. His voice is just barely able to be heard over the strong gusts.

"Sandstorm. At least that's what I think it is," Pelisus yells to Von.

"We need to find cover! Follow me!" Pelisus yells out to Von, grabbing his hand and pulling him along.

Pelisus and Von quickly head west, where there is a small tent close to a mile away. Von is only able to see it for a split second before the sand blowing behind them engulfs them. Pelisus has Von's hand gripped firmly to make sure they don't get separated. The strong winds in the desert make the small sand pellets feel like needles as they hit their skin. The only up side to the now-windy desert is it is no longer hot. When the two of them reach the tent, Pelisus pushes Von inside, following close behind and pulling the flap of leather over the entrance.

"How did you know about this place?" Von asks.

"Eagle eyes. I can look a mile in every direction," Pelisus replies.

"Interesting, just think … All I can do is swing a piece of metal around well," Von says with a slight chuckle.

"How long till the sandstorm ends?" Von asks.

"No idea. It could be a few hours," Pelisus replies.

Von looks around the inside of the tent to get a feel for his surroundings. The leather the tent is made out of what feels like some sort of animal skin. It's tough and heavy. A sword could rip through it easily, but the winds outside could never tear a hole in it. Anchoring the leather down to the ground are many large stakes all around the tent. Some of them look to be made of rock, others of metal, and some even of large branches. Whoever owns the tent must have lost some stakes over the years and had to create some of his or her of their own.

There is a small bed in the tent and a little wooden box that whoever lives here uses as a table. Aside from the bed and table, there is nothing else in the tent. With nothing to do as they wait for the sandstorm to dissipate, Von decides now would be a good time to catch up on some sleep. He sprawls himself out along the bed pad before closing his eyes and tilting his head back. Von slowly drifts off into a deep sleep while listening to the sounds of the winds whipping around outside.

"Von! Wake up! We're surrounded!" Pelisus yells out to Von.

Von jolts up out of bed and looks around the tent, only to notice that Pelisus isn't around. Without seeing Pelisus inside the tent, Von grabs his sword off the ground and dashes outside. When Von exits the tent, he raises his sword and is ready to fight whatever has Pelisus. Outside the tent, he is unable to see Pelisus. The sandstorm is still blowing violently, making it impossible for Von to see any more than a few feet in front of himself.

"Pelisus, where are you?" Von calls out to his friend.

Von stands still and listens for a response from Pelisus but doesn't hear one. Instead, in the distance he can hear a series of growls and barks. "Gnolls …" Von mumbles out loud before dashing toward the noises. As Von is running across the sand, a large gnoll tackles him to the ground, catching him off guard and disarming him. The gnoll raises its arm and brings its fist down toward Von's face. Von moves his head out of the way before returning the blow. Von makes contact with the gnoll's face, causing its grip to loosen.

This gives Von just enough time to crawl across the sand and grab his weapon. With his weapon in hand, he turns around and raises his sword to swing at the gnoll. Just as he reaches the peak of his swing and is about to bring his sword back down, another gnoll grabs his arm. Von swings his body around and uses his legs to knock the gnoll off his feet and to the ground. The gnolls releases its grip as it falls to the ground, giving Von the opportunity to swing again.

As he raises his sword, another gnoll tackles him to the ground as two more pin his arms to the ground. With Von's legs still free, he kicks wildly to ward off a few more gnoll attackers, until eventually he is overwhelmed. The gnoll he punched in the face earlier walks over to Von and gets payback. He plants his fists into both of Von's cheeks numerous times. Von's mouth fills with blood from accidentally biting the skin inside of his mouth during the beating. He waits for the gnoll to get close before spitting the blood into his face. This causes the gnoll to go berserk and relentlessly beat on Von's face with his two hands.

A few seconds in, Von is horribly dizzy and about to lose consciousness. But then out of nowhere, the sky above them lights up with red. The gnoll stops what he is doing and looks up into the sky, wondering what is going on.

"Nieuro Ferro," an unknown voice yells in the distance.

Everyone looks over to the east, where the voice came from but is unable to see anything through the sandstorm. When Von looks back up to the sky, he notices large fireballs raining down from above. The first one hits the gnoll that was just beating his face in. The gnoll shrieks in anguish as the fireball hits him. It almost completely burns through his flesh and immediately ignites his fur on fire. All of the other gnolls release their grip on Von and start to run to avoid any of the remaining fireballs.

Von lays his head back and closes his eyes, unable to keep conscious from the beating earlier. A few minutes later, Von re-awakes, with Pelisus being the first person he sees.

"That was a pretty nifty trick with those fireballs," Von mumbles to Pelisus.

"That wasn't me …" Pelisus says.

Von looks around and notices the sandstorm is now gone while pulling himself up and looking over Pelisus's shoulder. In the distance, Von spots his brother, Scarlet. The second he sees his brother, Von's eyes light up in anger. Von grabs his sword and rushes over to Scarlet, ready to cut him in two. With a slight chuckle, Scarlet raises his hand and sends a shockwave across the desert, knocking Von back and disarming him.

"That's not how you should treat your older brother, Von," Scarlet says with a chuckle.

"You son of a bitch! You killed those innocent people!" Von yells out to Scarlet.

"Ahh, I see you got some of your memory back. Too bad you're lying to yourself," Scarlet says, while tossing his hair to the side.

"What are you talking about?" Von shouts.

"Everything you know now is a lie! Your amnesia manipulated the events in your mind. You have yourself convinced that I am the bad guy, when in truth, I am far from it," Scarlet says to Von while pacing back and forth.

"Liar! You're just trying to manipulate me! Just like you did before!" Von yells out to Scarlet.

"Oh now, am I? Remember when you got admitted to the royal guard of Genisus? Think back, think hard. What did you do before that? What did you do afterward? You didn't do anything. The one who was in the royal guard was *me!*"

A look of shock crosses Von's face as he leans back trying to remember. "Yes, brother, remember the past. Remember who … you are …" Scarlet says to Von.

"Arrgh!" Von yells out as he brings both of his hands up to his head and grips it tightly. Memories rush into Von's head, different ones than before.

"Go back to that day where I got accepted into the royal guard. Tell me what you remember now."

Von can see a large stadium where the weekend arenas are held. Filling the stadium is a large crowd with Scarlet standing in the center, where the battles usually take place. Around Scarlet stand a few guards, all of whom are waiting for the king to come out to admit him into the Royal Guard. When the king steps foot onto the sand of the arena, the crowd goes wild. Von can remember trying to stand up on his seat to see over the tall person in front of him.

Unable to get a good enough look, he is forced to run through people and over to the edge, where he can get a perfect view of his brother.

"Scarlet, you are now a member of the Genisus Royal Guard. Do the city proud and protect it from all evil." Scarlet smiles to the king of Genisus and takes the sword before holding it up to the crowd around him. The crowd goes wild and cheers on Scarlet. After accepting the sword, Scarlet walks out of the arena where the king entered from. Von runs down a hallway nearby to meet Scarlet as he is exiting the arena.

"I'm so proud of you, big brother! I hope I grow up to be like you one day!" Von says to Scarlet.

Scarlet looks at his teenage brother and smiles. "You will. You'll be bigger than me one day. You will do great things with your life, Von. Mother and Father would be proud."

"Do you remember Von? Do you remember what really happened that day?" Scarlet says as Von grips his head in agony from the painful memories.

"Fine! But you still destroyed the village! You still killed all of those innocent people!" Von yells at Scarlet.

"Ha! Wrong! You destroyed that village! You killed all of those innocent people. I told you that you'd grow up to be big one day, brother … and you did—a monster!" Scarlet says to Von as he grips his head again, and new memories rush into his head.

The same vision from before where Von saw the village burning is now fresh in his head. The heat from the fire can be felt on Von's skin as he watches the village burn.

"Think harder, brother … Remember …." Scarlet says to him.

"Arrgh!" Von yells out as he starts to see more of the vision.

A young boy rides in the village on horseback. He is wearing silver-plated armor that gleams in the light of the sun. At his waist he has a sword that glows red. It shares a striking resemblance to the blue sword he has now. Von can't see his face, but it looks exactly like him. "Scarlet, your brother has returned!" a young woman yells out as she runs up to Von. When she gets too close to Von, he raises his sword and cuts her throat wide open. This causes blood to spray all over the ground around him. Scarlet comes running out of their childhood house and over to the wounded women lying on the ground.

"What have you done!" Scarlet yells out to his brother.

Von ignores Scarlet and continues to walk through the town. Everyone is at their windows looking out at Von as he walks through the town. When Von reaches the center of the town, he stands next to the well and extends his arms. He tilts his head up to the sky and yells out, "Nieuro Ferro." Von's eyes glow red as the sky changes in color. Fire rains down from the sky and ignites the whole town in flames. People run for cover as they are being burned alive.

"Brother … what have you done?" Scarlet yells out to Von.

Scarlet stands up and grabs a sword from the ground before running toward his brother. Von's hands are extended out toward the sky as he laughs wholeheartedly at the destruction around him. Scarlet runs up to Von and shoves the sword through his abdomen and out the backside before twisting it in the wound. Von grabs the sword in agony before smacking his brother across the face and knocking him away. Von pulls the sword out from his chest and collapses to the ground. Out of anger, Von grabs his sword off the ground and walks over to his brother.

Once standing over top of his brother, Von growls before raising his sword and using it to impale his brother to the ground. Von has one hand lightly placed around his wound while the other is gripping the sword that is holding his brother to the ground. Von leaves the sword in place and walks away from his brother. As he is walking away Von is able to see his own face amongst all the destruction this time, instead of his brother's.

"No … It can't be …" Von says out loud.

"Look at your chest, brother. Look at your scar …"

Von moves the tattered cloth out of the way and feels a long scar right below his ribcage. When he reaches around to his back, he feels a similar scar from the exit wound. "No … It can't be …" Von mumbles.

"Yes, brother. You killed those people! You're the evil one!" Scarlet says to Von before manically laughing.

"I must go now, brother. But we will meet again," Scarlet says before turning around and starting to walk away.

"Oh yeah, I almost forgot. Here you go, li'l bro." Scarlet turns around and throws a sword over to Von. It lands in the sand nearby.

After tossing the sword back to Von, Scarlet turns back around and phases out of reality. A mirror image of him jolts to the right hand side before he disappears completely. Von stands up and walks over to the sword, picking it up. The sword is identical to the blue one he already has, except this one has rubies instead of sapphires imbued into it. On the hilt of the sword there is an engraving that reads:

Use this sword well, brother.

—Scarlet

After reading the engraving, Von drops to his knees and stares down at the sword. Tears roll down the side of his face as he mumbles to himself, "I'm … I'm a monster …"

# Chapter 3
# Reawakening

With Scarlet now gone, Von is given the opportunity to take in everything. Even with the undeniable proof that Scarlet gave him, Von is still reluctant to believe that that is the truth. When he is able to finally gather himself enough to travel, Von and Pelisus continue through the desert. They pass their first oasis, which serves as a resting ground for a few minutes and a much-needed drink. They are also able to fill up their canteens for later use.

Pelisus struggles to try and talk to Von during the whole journey, but each and every time Pelisus tries to ask him a question, Von just ignores him. Von is having trouble understanding what he has seen in his visions, let alone trying to explain it to someone. The journey through the desert is long and rough for the two of them. After an hour of walking, each sand dune starts to feel like a whole mile, when it reality it is only a few hundred feet.

The extra weight they are carrying doesn't help either. Von does most of the work of dragging the burlap bag along while Pelisus leads the way. They both continue through the desert until nightfall, which is when Pelisus stops to make camp. Pelisus manages to locate a lonely tree in the desert. Among all the barren wasteland stands a single tree, a sign of life. Under this tree is where they make camp for the night.

They have to go without a fire this night, as there simply isn't enough wood around to start one. After they make the camp, Von lays awake and stares at the stars for hours. He falls asleep wondering if there was anyone else out there, anyone at all who was around when he supposedly attacked that village.

✦     ✦     ✦     ✦

"Von, Von, are you awake?" a young female voice asks him that he doesn't recognize.

"What? Where am I?" Von mumbles out loud as he sits up and looks around the room.

Von is lying on a bed in a small room. The young girl standing next to his bed has vibrant pink hair, not her natural color, of course. She has on almost identical clothing to Von, a tattered shirt and pants, giving Von the impression that she is a bit of a tomboy. Von looks at his hands and notices that they are clean and much smaller than they should be. When he reaches up and feels his face, he doesn't feel any facial hair present or growing. He can also feel a few pimples on his forehead, but luckily his hair perfectly covers them.

"You're in your house, silly!" the young girl yells out to Von.

"I must be dreaming …" Von mumbles out loud.

"Come on! Let's go play!" the young girl says to Von before grabbing his hand and pulling him out of the bed.

Von takes her hand and walks through the house with her. The house is made with solid wood. There is no drywall on the inside walls, so you are able to see the framework of the house. Along the outside of the house is solid brick. It was used to support the wood and keep the drafts out. The house is two stories tall, the perfect size for Von and his family of four.

"Where are we going?" Von asks the girl.

"To the forest!" the girl calls out.

When the two of them exit the house, Von realizes that he is in the village from his visions. As Von and the girl run through the town, everyone smiles and waves. The young girl leads Von out to the forest just outside of town before stopping.

"We're here!" she says out loud.

"Can I ask you something?" Von says out loud.

"Sure! Anything!" the girl yells out excitedly.

"What's your name?" Von asks.

"It's Lenya, silly! But today I want to be called Princess Lenya!" Lenya says with a smile.

"And you are my knight in shining armor, Sir Von Lockfur," Lenya says before prancing off into the woods.

Von goes numb and stares off into the woods. "Sir Von Lockfur ..." he mumbles to himself repeatedly. "Is this why I thought I was a real knight?" Von asks himself.

"Are you coming, Von?" Lenya yells out to Von.

Von nods and catches up to Lenya before following her further into the forest. Lenya finally stops when she reaches a small clearing in the forest. This is the only place in the forest anywhere close to town that the light is able to shine through the trees and to the ground. When Von seen Lenya standing in the light with her hair glistening, he knows that he is in love. There has to be a connection between the two of them. If Von felt this way about her, she must know the truth of what happened that day. Von runs over to Lenya and stands in the clearing with her.

"Okay, now you're going to be the knight in shining armor that protects me and my village from harm!" Lenya says to Von.

"Who plans to harm the village?" Von asks, trying to ignore the irony.

"Don't play stupid, Von," a strange voice echoes throughout Von's head.

"What?" Von says out loud.

"Tell that poor girl the truth. Tell her that you killed her family. Tell her you killed every single person that she knew or loved. You betrayed her trust."

"Scarlet, is that you?" Von asks.

"Ha ha ha, how did you know?" Scarlet asks.

"Because you're the only one who believes that I destroyed the village," Von says to himself.

"I am sorry you feel that way. Here, I'll tell you what. If you pass my test, then I will tell you where Lenya is."

"And if I don't?"

"She dies."

Von walks over to the forest and picks up a large and sturdy stick before returning to Lenya's side. A smirk comes across Von's face as he looks up through the clearing and into the sky before saying, "Bring it." Manic laughter echoes through the woods, scaring Lenya and causing her to grab a hold of Von's arm. Movement can be heard in the woods around them while silhouettes of rats start to burst out from the forest.

Their bodies are black aside from their eyes, which are glowing yellow. Von crushes the rats that come out of the forest and makes sure that Lenya stays behind him at all times. It only takes one strong downward swing to kill one of the rats. Their bodies split in half from the force of the swings. When one of the rats is killed, its body disappears right before their eyes. After all the rats are dead, Von looks up through the clearing and shouts out to Scarlet, "Is that all you have?"

Without a response, Von hears more rustling in the bushes around him. He grips his stick tightly while waiting for whatever it is to show itself. The rustling is faint at first, but it quickly grows and even forms a pattern. Von listens closely and hears, "Thump thump, thump thump, thump thump, thump thump." It sounds like a very large creature that is carrying a lot of weight coming toward Von and Lenya.

Before the beast shows itself, a chilling roar can be heard, sounding like that of a bear. Von grips his stick tightly and propels himself in front of Lenya as the bear bursts out from the forest. Just like the rats, the bear is nothing but a silhouette. The bear stands five feet tall when it's on all fours and ten feet when it arches its body up, the height of which only a Kodiak could reach.

Von takes the first swing and hits the beast with his stick across the face. As expected, it only infuriates the beast. The bear takes a swing at Von and strikes him to the ground. He rolls out of the way to avoid the bear's claws before getting back up onto his feet.

"What is this, some kind of sick joke, Scarlet? You know I can't beat this thing!" Von yells out as he prepares for the bears next attack.

The bear swings its giant paw at Von, which he easily dodges. Dodging the attack, he brings his stick down as hard as he can over top of the bear's nose, but just like before, it only pisses him off. The bear retaliates with another swing, which hits Von and knocks him across the ground. He loses a hold of his stick as he comes into contact with the tough ground below. The bear ignores Von and turns its attention to Lenya. It stands up tall and lets out a triumphant roar before slowly walking toward Lenya.

Lenya is curled up next to a tree, crying. She is unable to understand what is going on. Von shakes off the blow and rolls over to look at the bear. As he watches it go toward Lenya, his eyes light up with anger.

"Use it, Von, use your *bloodlust!*" Scarlet yells out to him.

Von grabs the stick off the ground and squeezes it so tight that he can hear it start to crack.

"Channel your anger into the weapon, Von. Channel it!" Scarlet yells out.

Von nods and diverts his anger into the stick. As he does this, the stick begins to faintly grow red. Von has his teeth clamped together and his lips parted. Just like the stick, his eyes begin to glow faintly red. As his anger builds and he channels more of it into the stick, the color gets darker, as do his eyes. Von snaps out of his trance and screams at the top of his lungs before rushing toward the bear.

He leaps into the air and onto the bear's back while swinging the stick wildly at the bear. Once on top of the bear, Von relentlessly beats it with the stick. Each of Von's swings comes into contact with the bear's skull. After a few seconds of Von's relentless pummeling, the bear's skull can be heard cracking. A few seconds, later the bear's lifeless body collapses to the ground. It wasn't even given a chance to fight back. As the bear lies across the ground, Von continues to pummel it, unable to break out of his trance.

"Congratulations, Von, you passed," Scarlet says to him.

"Now, where is she?" Von yells out as he jolts awake.

Pelisus quickly tilts his head up and looks around after Von shouts. "What's going on?" Pelisus asks Von. Von stands up and looks at the desert around him. The only thing lighting up the desert all around him is the moon and the stars. Without seeing anyone around aside from Pelisus, Von runs to the tallest sand dune nearby and stands on top. He looks up at the moon and throws his arms out to each of his sides before screaming at the top of his lungs.

"Scarlet, where is she?"

Von collapses to his knees to catch his breath as Pelisus runs over to him. Pelisus stops next to Von and kneels down. "Are you okay?" Pelisus asks Von. Von nods to Pelisus, instead of talking, as he tries to hold in his tears.

"Cathunder," a voice whispers into Von's head.

"Cathunder?" Von asks himself out loud.

"What about it?" Pelisus asks.

"That is where they're holding Lenya."

"Who is Lenya?"

"She is a friend … We should go. Do you know where Cathunder is?"

"Of course I do. The gnolls and dark elves have a shared friendship," Pelisus replies.

"Take me to Cathunder. I need to find Lenya," Von says to Pelisus.

Pelisus nods before turning around and pointing in the opposite direction. "Cathunder is a few miles in that direction. If we move quickly, we can reach it by sun up."

Von stands up, nods, and says, "Then let's get a move on."

They both go back to the tree and collect the supplies they brought with them before walking west toward Cathunder. Von holds both of his swords tightly in his hands, ready to kill anything that gets between him and Cathunder. Even though Von only knows the general direction in which he must travel, he is the one in the lead. His anger and love for Lenya drive him forward at a quickened pace. All through the night they travel, over and across the Western Desert.

Travel at night was much easier for them. Instead of the sun roasting them, the moon lit their way. The sand is much cooler at night, which actually makes it feel good against the blisters on their feet from the hot sand during the day. Everything around them is so peaceful and serene. No sounds could be heard other than each of their footsteps and the burlap sack dragging against the ground.

It took Von and Pelisus until sunup to reach Cathunder. Cathunder is a large city, part underground and part above ground. Originally Cathunder was just a cave, which the gnolls expanded into a large city. As their population grew and they had more visitors, it quickly expanded into a whole above-ground section as well. The city's walls are made of sand so strongly compacted that it became solid. The gnolls also used some sort of glue on the walls to keep it together. Rumors over the years are that gnoll saliva mixed with sand formed their solution. The gnolls keep it as their little secret.

Running through the center of Cathunder underground is a stream. It is said to flow from the Swamps of Elous out into the Banished Sea, far to the north. The stream is what the gnolls use as their drinking water. The many miles it travels underground from the swamps almost perfectly purifies it by the time it reaches Cathunder. Von and Pelisus come over the last sand dune before stopping and looking down at Cathunder.

At the front of Cathunder there is a large sandy gate leading into the city. Pelisus informs Von that during the night the gnolls always close the gate but during the day they leave it open. The large sand walls that circle Cathunder have dozens of gnoll sentries perched along them, all with torches to light up the night. Getting close enough for them to see you would be suicide. The two men kneel down and discuss a possible attack strategy.

"For you to try and enter would be suicide," Pelisus says to Von.

"I'm not going to let her die in there," Von adds.

"I'll go in and get her then," Pelisus says.

"What are you talking about?" Von asks.

"The dark elves and gnolls are friendly with each other. We even share a town to the southeast. I'll offer to buy the slave girl from them, and then I will walk out here with her, both of us unharmed," Pelisus says.

"I guess we really don't have any other options, huh?" Von asks Pelisus.

"No, we don't. This is our only one," Pelisus says.

"How will you know which girl it is?"

"Think about her right now," Pelisus replies.

Von looks up and to the right as he remembers Lenya. A smile comes across his face as thoughts of when they were kids burst into his mind. Pelisus watches Von and casts a spell to read his mind. Upon casting the spell, Pelisus's eyes twitch as he is temporarily infused with Von's memories.

"I got it. Young girl, pink hair, named Lenya. I'll find your friend," Pelisus says to Von.

"What should I do if you're not back before noon?" Von asks.

"Run, because by then they will surely be after you," Pelisus replies.

"Go in with swords swinging, got it," Von says while smirking.

Pelisus smiles and throws the hood of his cloak over top of his head before starting the long walk toward the city. Von lies back on the sand dune and stares up at the sky, not being able to do much more than wait while Pelisus enters the city.

As Pelisus walks up to the front gate, the gnolls spot him. They wait patiently to see who he is first before shooting, having recognized his cloak. Pelisus stops in front of the gate and removes his hood before looking up at the gnoll sentry.

"I am Archmage Pelisus of Terrova. I seek entry into Cathunder, for I have matters with the king."

As Pelisus speaks, the gnolls above growl and bark at each other, discussing if they should let Pelisus into the city. A few minutes go by before the gnolls open the front doors to the city. When the sandy doors grind against the sandy ground, Von pops up from his sand dune and watches Pelisus enter. Once inside, Pelisus puts his hood back on and walk toward the underground section of Cathunder, where the king is.

While Pelisus walks through the city, all of the gnoll sentries watch him closely. They've never had any dark elves in their town aside from traders. Having a very powerful wizard arrive at this time of night wanting to speak with the king aroused many interests. On his way to the castle, Pelisus walks by the area where they hold the prisoners. He looks into each cell but doesn't see Lenya anywhere.

A look of dread crosses Pelisus's face after pacing the holding cells. If the gnolls don't have Lenya there. Where could she be? When Pelisus reaches the castle, the guards force him to wait out front until the king is ready to see him. The castle of Cathunder is in the deepest section of the underground city.

The gnolls created a whole new cave specifically for their castle. It stands almost one hundred feet tall, and unlike the rest of the city, it is made of brick. Flowing right through the middle of the castle is the underground river that the whole city uses for drinking water. The castle was built at the furthest point downstream of the river. This was done to prevent the townsfolk from thinking their water was being tampered with from inside of the castle.

Of course, this also created other problems, like someone wanting to poison the king. For such reasons, there was a system engineered for purifying the water when it reached the castle.

Pelisus stood outside the castle for close to fifteen minutes until his escort arrived to take him inside to see the king. The inside of the castle was much different than the one he was used to in Terrova. Instead of everything being golden and gleaming in the light, there was loose sand everywhere. The whole floor was covered with a very thin layer of sand. But what else could you expect from a kingdom being run by gnolls?

The escort leads Pelisus up to the throne and tells him to wait there until the king arrives. Pelisus nods before looking around and admiring the castle that the gnolls built. Even though it is dirty, there are still many impressive things to see, like the solid stone chandelier hanging from the ceiling or the life-size statue of their king. Pelisus's wait this time around isn't that long. Within five minutes, the king came walking into the throne room from his corridor.

"To what do I owe your visit?" the king asks Pelisus.

"I've gotten word that you have a slave girl that I am interested in buying," Pelisus says to the king.

"May I ask, what interest do you have in her?" the king asks.

"Purely personal, I assure you," Pelisus replies.

The king nods to Pelisus. "What is this slave's name, and how do you know that we have her?"

"Word from an outsider said that you recently captured their village to the north and have taken her hostage. Her name is Lenya," Pelisus says to the king.

"Yes, yes, I know Lenya. She works directly under me in the castle. She is one of my best," the king says to Pelisus.

"May I ask how long you've had her for?" Pelisus asks curiously.

"Close to a year now. I think she kind of likes it here. I will have to discuss you taking her with a few others. And I assure you, the price will be steep," the king says to Pelisus.

Pelisus smiles and nods. "I'll buy a room at the inn. Just let me know when you've made up your mind."

Pelisus pulls his hood over top of his head and slightly bows to the king before walking away. As Pelisus is leaving the room, the king's guard captain approaches him. The king leans over and whispers into his ear, "Find that dark elf and throw him into the jail cells. I think we have ourselves a new slave."

Pelisus walks through the city to find the closest inn. He notices that none of the citizens are making eye contact with him. Each of them turn away or run inside of their houses as he passes. They're obviously trying to avoid him. Pelisus can tell something is going on. The scent of betrayal is in the air. Pelisus arrives at the inn, and a guard approaches him and tells him that the king has made up his mind. He offers to escort Pelisus back to the castle. When Pelisus declines, the gnoll informs him that declining isn't an option.

Pelisus nods to the gnoll before following him back toward the castle. On route back to the castle, Pelisus sends a shockwave directly at the gnoll's head and knocks him unconscious. With the gnoll out of the way, Pelisus runs back toward the castle to find Lenya. As Pelisus runs toward the castle, another one of the guards sent for him discovers the unconscious gnoll on the ground. The guard yells out to all the other gnolls in the city to raise the alarm.

⊕　　⊕　　⊕　　⊕

Meanwhile, Von is still out lying on the sand dune and staring up at the sky. The night is so peaceful until he heard a loud gong go off repeatedly from inside of Cathunder. Knowing that Pelisus's cover was blown Von stands up, grabs his swords, and sprints toward the front gates of the city. Each of the gnolls from on top the wall are now gone, as they are all flooding toward the castle to help protect the king.

When Von gets close enough to the front gates, he jumps up and shoves both of his swords through it. He uses both of his swords as if they were ice picks to climb up the gate. When he gets close enough to the top, he throws one of his swords over before pulling the other one out and jumping down. On the other side, he grabs his other weapon and sprints toward the underground portion of the city.

In the underground portion of Cathunder, Von starts to catch up to a long line of gnolls heading toward the castle. The second they see Von, they stop running toward the castle and surround him. Von holds both of his swords casually as the gnolls get closer and closer to him. Just before they attack, a smirk comes across Von's face as he asks them, "You sure you want to do this?"

The gnolls growl and bark while dashing toward Von. Von races toward one of the gnolls and blocks its attack, catapulting himself over it. While in midair, he thrusts the sword through the back of the gnoll, splitting its spine in two and killing it instantly. The second he lands, Von does a back flip to avoid the incoming two swings from behind him. At the peak of the back flip, he twirls the swords in both hands around and slices through the gnolls that are at his sides.

When he lands, he quickly spins around and thrusts both of his weapons forward through another gnoll. His swords are still inside of the gnoll, and he twists them to turn them horizontally. With just a snap of his wrists, he tears the swords through the gnoll's body, leaving the gnoll's bottom half detached from its upper half. With his swords now free, Von does a whirlwindlike motion with both of his weapons, making sure that nothing is around him. Unluckily for Von, all of the gnolls are able to dodge this attack.

Two gnolls dash forward toward Von. The first comes from in front and the second from his left-hand side. Von raises his right hand up above his head and brings the sword down as hard as he possibly can over the gnoll in front of him, splitting the gnoll's skull wide open and getting his sword wedged between the eye sockets. The gnoll coming up on his left is quickly finished off by a quick thrust to the chest.

Von spins around and looks forward at the remaining gnolls. The sword from his right hand is still wedged in the skull of the gnoll. When the gnolls get close enough, Von kicks the body into them, with his sword still in it. The attack catches them off guard and knocks a lot of them to the ground. Some of them it even disarms, causing their swords to fly through the air. Von dashes forward with his sword swinging wildly, cutting through anything it comes into contact with.

Von kills any gnolls that come in his way until he can reach his other sword. From having kicked the body across the room, he weakened the hold on his sword, allowing him to easily take it back. Now that he has both of his weapons back, he gets ready for round two. Von takes care of all the approaching gnolls with quick and efficient slashes across the chest, followed by a killing blow across the back of the neck once they've bent over from the pain.

After Von finishes off all the gnolls around him, he continues toward the castle. He is occasionally forced to take out gnolls that get in his way and try to stop him. Generally he doesn't even have to stop in order to get by them. A quick thrust into their chest or a downward slice to their neck while running by is efficient enough. As Von gets closer to the castle, he can hear a large amount of commotion and the sound of a young girl screaming.

Right outside the castle are Pelisus and Lenya. They are both fighting off any gnolls that get near them when Von arrives. Von sees that they are in danger and rushes forward into the pack of gnolls. Having the advantage of them all facing away from him works in his favor; he cuts through them like a hot knife through butter. With Von laying waste to the gnolls from behind and Pelisus shooting fireballs at them from the front, they don't stand a chance. Less than a minute after Von arrives, all of the gnolls are dead.

With all the gnolls dead, Von pauses and looks up at Lenya. When she turns to him, their eyes lock in perfect synchronicity. A

sharp pain rips across Von's forehead before everything goes black and he falls to the ground.

"Where … where am I?"

Von stands up and looks around. Everything is black around him. There is no ground, there are no objects. It is just an empty, seemingly endless void.

"What … What is going on?"

Moments later, Von finds himself on top of a rooftop, looking back when he was younger, around the age of ten. Lenya is there too. They are back in their hometown, the one that Scarlet, or Von, destroyed years ago.

"Von …" Lenya says out loud.

"Yes?" Von asks.

"You leave tomorrow, right, for Genisus?"

Von nods to Lenya without saying a word.

"Everyone is trying to leave this town …" Lenya says to Von.

"But I'm not like those other people. I'm going to do something; I want to join the Royal Guard," Von says to Lenya.

"I don't know how long it will be until I can come back and see you, Lenya …"

"If you do well … how will I know?" Lenya asks.

Von puts his head down and shrugs, not knowing how to answer her question.

"Hey, why don't we make a promise?" Lenya asks Von.

"If I'm ever in trouble, I want my hero to come and save me. Von … I want you to come and save me," Lenya says.

"I will Lenya … I promise," Von says to Lenya with a smile

Lenya smiles and places her head on Von's shoulder closing her eyes. Von leans his head against hers, staring up into the sky at the stars.

"Von, Von! Wake up! We've got to get out of here!" Pelisus says to Von, shaking him awake.

Von shakes his head side to side, pulling himself up onto his feet. He looks over to Lenya and smiles. After all this time and almost a year as a slave in Cathunder, she still has her vibrant pink hair. Her face is much prettier than Von had remembered; it was almost that of an angel. Lenya's brown eyes flow very well with the black bow in her hair.

"Von! You're alive!" Lenya calls out before running up to Von and throwing her arms around him.

Lenya leans back and looks Von in the face before asking, "So you remembered … the promise?"

A slight smile comes across Von's face as he nods and says, "Yes."

Von puts his arms around Lenya and gently pats her on the back before saying, "I missed you so much …"

"Not to be a mood kill here, but we need to get going," Pelisus says.

Von nods to Pelisus and motions Lenya and him to follow. After the large battle at the castle, mostly all of the gnoll guards have been killed or are hiding to prevent being killed. This makes it very easy to escape out of the city with no more bloodshed. Once they make it out of the underground portion of Cathunder, they find someone waiting for them. Standing by the front gates leading back out into the Western Desert is Scarlet.

"Well, well, brother, I see you have found Lenya, your childhood sweetheart," Scarlet says to Von.

"You're not walking away from me this time, Scarlet!" Von yells out.

"Ha, ha, ha … It's not that easy, Von. It will take more than your sense of humor to kill me. But now that you insist … I want you to head north, over the Land Bridge, and meet me in the town of Ethun. If you don't remember where it is, surely someone else will. From there, I will give you more of a direction. See you soon, Von," Scarlet says to Von.

"Oh yes, and about this gate blocking your way out to the desert. I will fix it for you."

Scarlet turns around and sticks his hand out toward the gate. A shroud of light flickers around his hand before one side of the gate is blown into hundreds of pieces.

"I shall see you soon, brother," Scarlet says, disappearing before their eyes.

"We've already spent too much extra time here, we need to go," Pelisus says.

Von and Lenya nod to Pelisus before following him out of Cathunder and north through the Western Desert. All three of them run as much as they can for the next few hours until the sun is on the horizon. The further north they get, the more lush and green the landscape gets. Instead of just sand, they start to see bushes every once in awhile, then two bushes, groups of bushes, a cactus or two, eventually even some desert trees.

By morning, they made it far enough north to find the large river that separates the two main continents of Drylor. Hundreds of years ago, the two continents of Drylor were separate. But many years ago, the elves and humans decided to create a large bridge to span between them. This would make trading between their allies, the gnomes and dwarves to the south, much easier. The Land Bridge took almost fifty years to complete. They had to make it close to two miles long in order to span all the way over the Great River.

Once the Land Bridge was finished, the orcs and ogres wanted to use it as well. They had a much different use in mind, though. Their intentions were to raid the towns on the other side and take whatever they wanted. So the humans and elves brought their forces to the bridge and waged a war against the orcs and ogres. The battle was short; it only lasted a single night. Ultimately, in the end it was a tie. The orcs and ogres kept the southern half of the bridge while the elves and humans kept the northern half.

The war camps on each end of the bridge were made into towns after the war. The humans and elves named theirs Ethun and Espium while the orcs and ogres named theirs Ferrundas and Hiberon. After all the years of the rival towns existing on both ends of the bridge, there has never been another war or even a single fight. However, the orcs and ogres will not let anyone pass from the south, nor will the elves and humans let any orcs or ogres continue to the north. Getting across the Land Bridge will be tricky, if at all possible.

The sun is up in the morning sky as the three of them arrive at the Great River, just west of the Land Bridge. All three of them, still exhausted from the run, decide to stop next to the river to get a drink and take a break.

"We should make camp here, and rest," Pelisus says while drinking from the river.

"We won't be able to cross the Land Bridge until nighttime anyway. The guards will be able to easily see us in the daylight," Pelisus says.

Everyone nods to Pelisus, splitting up and searching for wood for a fire. While collecting the wood, Von slowly makes his way over to Lenya. He tries to make it look as casual as possible and not intentional at all, but Lenya caught on.

"Hey, Lenya … did I ever come back to the town we grew up in?"

"You mean Milem?"

"Yeah, that is the name."

"About five years ago, you came back to see me. Your brother came that day too …"

Von's face goes pale as he swallows hard, reluctant to ask the next question.

"What happened that day?"

"You really … don't remember do you?"

"Your brother destroyed the village … You tried to stop him but …" Lenya adds.

"But what?" Von asks curiously.

"But … you died …"

"I what?" Von asks shockingly.

"You died … You died in my arms Von… I felt your heart stop … I felt you stop breathing … That scar on your chest … Your brother shoved a sword through you and impaled you on the ground. That is where you died," Lenya says to Von.

Von reaches down and unties his shirt to run his hand across the scar. A chill runs through him as he touches the scar and vaguely remembers being impaled on the ground. Everything Scarlet told him happened was reversed. Scarlet wasn't the one to attack Von; Von was the one to attack Scarlet. Scarlet cast the spell and destroyed the village. That doesn't explain how Von is alive, though.

"I tried—trust me, I tried to pull the sword out and drag you away—but the fire was too strong. You told me to save myself. The fire was too strong … I had to leave you there, Von. Trust me, if I had known you were alive …" Lenya says to Von.

"How many years ago was this?" Von asks Lenya.

"Five."

Von picks up the last stick off the ground and starts to walk back toward the pile that Pelisus has started at the campsite. He drops all of the sticks he was carrying into the pile before sitting down and staring at the wood. Lenya and Pelisus both walk up at the same time with two more loads of sticks and drop them into the pile. Pelisus extends his hand and ignites the fire before sitting down.

"We should probably get some rest since we will have to cross the Land Bridge at night," Pelisus says to everyone.

Von nods to Pelisus without saying a word. He kicks his legs out from underneath him and sprawls out across the ground. When Von looks in front of him, he is able to see Lenya sitting at the campfire. A smile comes across his face before he closes his eyes and falls asleep.

"Von, hey, Von, wake up! We need to get a move on if we want to cross the Land Bridge tonight," Lenya says while shaking Von awake.

Von lifts his head up off the ground and looks around. It is dark out. Pelisus and Lenya are both already up and getting ready to leave. Lenya is tasked with waking Von, while Pelisus is putting out the fire.

"It is about a two-hour hike east and another hour to cross the Land Bridge once we figure out how to get onto it," Pelisus says as he finishes putting out the fire.

Von stands up and grabs both of his swords before nodding to Pelisus, letting him know that he is ready to go. Pelisus throws his hood over top of his head, walking east toward the Land Bridge. Just like the other night in the desert, it is nice and cool. With the sun now down, the desert sand is given a chance to cool off and actually feels quite soothing on your feet.

Walking alongside of the river, they are able to see quite a bit of wildlife. A lot of the animals have their homes in the nearby bushes or trees, close to a water source. When they get close enough, they can sometimes hear the animals run off into a nearby bush or tree to hide. But most of the time they can't hear anything over the sound of the roaring river to the north. The river is rapid; the water is flowing at a dangerous pace.

If anyone tried to cross it on foot or even with a sturdy boat, they would most likely drown. It takes them two hours to reach the outskirts of a town by the Land Bridge, just as Pelisus predicted. The three of them take refuge behind a rock right outside of Hiberon, the orc and ogre town. Stationed all around the walls of the town are orcish archers. Just like Cathunder, getting close with all those guards around would be suicide.

"I take it as you can't bribe them to let us cross, huh, Pelisus?" Von asks.

"That didn't work too well last time. I think our best bet is to sneak across somehow," Pelisus says.

The three of them circle around the town of Hiberon to the front of the Land Bridge. The Land Bridge is blocked off by a giant wooden wall with a gate in the center. All along the wall there are more orcish archers with torches to light up the night. The wall runs all the way across the Land Bridge, from Hiberon to Ferrundas. The orcish side of the wall is very demonic. At the bottom of the wall there are large white spikes that were built into the wood. They're at least four feet long, and their points gleam in the moonlight.

All along the railings on top of the wall there are also large spikes. These are much shorter than the ones on the ground but look to be as equally as painful if touched.

Every twenty feet along the wall, there is an orcish archer stationed to watch both sides of the gate, making sure that no one passes at any time. In front of the gate they also have patrols that walk back and forth all throughout the night, in case anyone does manage to get close to the gate when an orc isn't paying attention. After seeing the level of security they have at the gate, passing would be almost impossible.

"We're never going to be able to get through there. We need to think of another option," Von says to Pelisus.

"I've heard stories of a secret bridge down below, but I've never met someone who has seen it or crossed it," Pelisus replies.

"It looks like that will be our only option. Can you take us there?" Von asks.

"Well, I don't really know where it is, but I guess I can try and locate it."

Pelisus stands up and quickly walks back west, toward Hiberon. The three of them do a very large circle around Hiberon, being very careful to stay out of the guards' line of site. They arrive back at the rock they hid behind earlier.

"Okay, so under this side of the Land Bridge there is said to be a ladder that leads to a rope that you can shimmy across to a bridge," Pelisus says.

"Well, I'm glad this is going to be easy," Von says sarcastically.

"Hey, compared to up there, this *is* the easy way across!" Lenya says jokingly.

Pelisus runs out from behind the rock and over to the first large pillar that holds the land bridge up. The pillar is made from a giant type of tree; it is roughly five feet perfectly round. All around the pillar is sand and rock, making up the shoreline next to the river below. Pelisus feels around the pillar but doesn't feel anything they could use as a ladder. Von and Lenya follow him over to the second pillar and wait for him to search it as well. Still Pelisus has no luck with the second pillar.

They follow him over to the third and final pillar before the water's edge. Pelisus feels around the pillar but doesn't feel anything. He looks over at Von and Lenya before saying, "It may be on the other side, but that is a two-mile walk, or more. We don't have time to take that ladder and cross the Land Bridge too."

"Well once we're on the Land Bridge, we don't have to worry about being seen right?" Von asks Pelisus.

"*You* don't have to worry about being seen. I am not going to be able to cross the elvish side without being stopped. I am a dark elf after all," Pelisus replies.

Von nods before walking over to the large wood pillar that Pelisus just checked for a ladder. He feels around where Pelisus did and gets the same outcome. He looks straight up and walks around the pillar to see if he can see anything above. On the northern side of the pillar, Von spots a rope all the way up at the top, right under the bridge.

"Look! Up there!" Von says, pointing to the rope.

Lenya and Pelisus both look up and see the rope above them. "Well, I guess we know that we're on the right side," Pelisus says.

"Yeah, but there is no ladder … So how do we get up?" Pelisus asks.

"Are you sure you heard right and people didn't bring their own ladders?" Lenya asks.

While Lenya and Pelisus are talking, Von continues to investigate the pillar. He looks for any clues that could explain how people get up it and to the rope that is above them.

"I am positive. I've heard the stories dozens of times. No one ever said you needed to bring your own ladder," Pelisus says to Lenya.

"Well, I think they're called stories for a reason," Lenya says sarcastically.

"I guess you're right …" Pelisus says before being interrupted by Von.

"Hey guys, I think I found something," Von calls out.

Von jumps up and grabs onto a large metal spike coming out of the side of the pillar. Once he has a hold of it, he uses his feet to push his body up to almost eye level with the spike. He uses his other arm and reaches around the other side of the pillar to find another spike to grab onto. Once he finds it, he pulls himself up until he finds two more. Now that he is standing up with his chest pressed against the pillar, he looks back and smiles.

"There are spikes attached to the side of the pillar. That's the ladder," Von says to Lenya and Pelisus.

As Von continues to climb up the side of the pillar, Pelisus and Lenya try to pull themselves up to grab onto the second spike. With neither of them being strong enough, they find a large rock they can stand on, which helps them make the first and second spike much easier. Von reaches the top, where he can see the long rope that runs across to a bridge.

"Getting across this rope is going to take a lot of stamina. Do you guys have it in you?" Von asks Lenya and Pelisus.

"I hope so," Pelisus replies as he climbs up the spikes on the side of the pillar.

Von looks down the rope and notices that it is slanting very slightly downward. He ever so slightly leans back and pulls off his leather tunic. Once he manages to get off his tunic, he tosses it over the rope and grabs onto both sides of it. Afterward, he jumps off the pillar and lets momentum do the work, carrying him down to the bridge.

Pelisus and Lenya watch Von as he slides down the rope, making it look so easy. Before Pelisus goes across the rope, Lenya looks up to him and asks, "Pelisus, can I go with you? My clothing is too thin to hold my weight, and your robe is thick enough to hold both of us."

"Yeah sure, try and climb up here and hop onto my back," Pelisus says to Lenya.

Lenya climbs up the last few spikes and gets ready to jump onto the back of Pelisus. "You ready?" Pelisus asks Lenya.

"Mmhmm," Lenya ever so slightly mumbles before putting both of her arms around Pelisus's neck. Pelisus steps off of the pillar and slides down the rope toward the bridge. Below them is the roaring river. Even through the darkness of the night they can see the rapids white foam below them. If they lost a hold of the robe or the rope snapped, they would most certainly fall to their death.

Von is waiting for them as they land on the bridge. "Glad you made it," Von says with a smile. They start their way down the bridge, which runs parallel to the Land Bridge above. The small bridge they are on is made of thin planks of wood, just big enough to hold their weight. Shockingly, the bridge doesn't blow in the wind that much. Every hundred or so feet, there is a large pillar that holds the Land

Bridge, above them up. The small bridge they are on is anchored to these pillars and also wraps around them.

At every pillar there is a set of torches and lanterns, sometimes even a small roll-up bed and a few crates of supplies. They must have belonged to people passing through or elves that occasionally come down here to service the bridge. Even though the bridge above them was blocking out most of the moonlight, they could still easily see where they were going. Just enough light got through the cracks of the bridge to light their way.

Walking underneath the bridge, all three of them were careful not to talk. If there were any guards up above, they didn't want to alert them of their presence. They walked for roughly forty-five minutes before they saw the shoreline on the other side of the bridge. Unlike the last shoreline, this one was much different. It consisted of rock and gravel rather than sand and rock. This side of the bridge was also much different. At the end of the bridge there is a ladder leading down to the ground below. There was no puzzle to figure out or rope for them to climb across.

Von was the first one down the ladder. Once at the bottom, Von looked around to make sure everything was safe before waving Pelisus and Lenya down. He helped Pelisus and Lenya safely off the ladder, leading everyone out from under the Land Bridge and over toward the elvish town of Ethun, where Scarlet asked to meet him. Ethun was a short walk away, only a few minutes. While walking to Ethun, Von notices that this side of the river is vastly different than the other side.

Instead of sand, everything is dirt. Also, every few feet there are small patches of grass. To the north, Von could see large hills covered in grass at least three or more feet tall. To the west are the Ochre Plains. The Ochre Plains' grass has a golden tint to it and stood out among all the other grass. In the Ochre Plains, it seemed like it was fall all year round.

As the three of them got closer to Ethun, they could see smoke from the city billowing up into the sky. The smell of burning flesh filled the air as Von's eyes glazed over with anger. As they close in on the city, it became more and more obvious what Scarlet had done.

The gates to the city were destroyed. There were large amounts of blood all over the walls, as well as small chunks of flesh. As the three of them stepped into the city, the things they are exposed to only becomes worse. Bodies are torn in two in the middle of the street, with their intestines hanging out of the upper half. Birds have already found their way over to the bodies and started to feast on them. Each of the wooden poles that were used to hold a torch to light the paths now has a body impaled on it. You can tell whoever did this took his time and enjoyed it.

As they continue to walk through the city, Pelisus spots a message written in blood on the tallest building. The building is made of stone and is as smooth as possible. This made it the perfect building for Scarlet to choose. When Pelisus notices the message, he taps Von on the shoulder and points it out to him. Von looks over; his already hate-filled eyes fill with even more. The message read:

Von

It was short and simple. The message wasn't really what bothered Von. The fact that Scarlet dedicated destroying a whole village specifically to Von is what bothered him the most.

"So is that what he brought us here for? The only purpose was to see the outcome of his sick little game?" Von says.

Von looks up into the sky and throws his arms out at his sides before screaming at the top of his lungs, "*You better keep running, Scarlet … Because when I find you, I'm going to kill you …*"

"So what are we supposed to do now?" Lenya asks Pelisus.

"Well, now that we're here … We might as well collect some supplies and spend what's left of the night," Pelisus replies.

"Von, are you okay?" Lenya asks.

"Yeah … I'm fine. Let's get some weapons and armor and spend the night," Von says to Lenya.

Von walks away from Lenya and Pelisus before they are able to say anything else. He walks over to the edge of the town and stares out at the Ochre Plains to the west. Witnessing what his brother has done to Ethun, he needs a few minutes to clear his mind.

"Should we go talk to him?" Lenya asks Pelisus.

"No. Give him a few minutes. He will come around," Pelisus replies.

Pelisus walks over to the armor and weapons shop nearby. The building is mostly still intact, aside from the front door being smashed in and severe structural damage around the frame of the door. The inside of the building is mostly still intact. When the door was knocked out of its frame so violently, the building shook, knocking some of the items off of their shelves.

The floor was covered in loose armor and weapons. This made it difficult for Lenya and Pelisus to find what they wanted. After a few minutes of searching, Pelisus picks up a very large wooden quarterstaff. The quarterstaff is a windy piece of wood. It was most likely a root of a once very large tree. At the top of the quarterstaff, the wood coils around and is held together by an emerald gemstone. Pelisus holds the piece of wood above his head and swings it around a few times to get a feel of it. Swinging it around over his head, he brings it down with a powerful thrust in front of him.

Pelisus smiles and says, "This is all I'll need."

Pelisus starts to look for some armor that will fit Von, while Lenya continues to search the building for two daggers that meet her standards. Lenya finally finds two very small daggers, about a foot and a half in length. The grip on the daggers is just barely big enough to fit her very small hands, since the blades make up the biggest portion of the weapon. The blade of the weapon is about ten inches long and in the shape of a pyramid.

The blade is large and fat at the bottom but shrinks into a small point the further away from the hilt it gets. The first four inches of the blade off of the hilt have a gap, forming a perfect triangle. At the end of this gap, there is a small sliver of metal embedded into the blade with a more grayish color. The gap in the blade almost fits the design perfectly and in no way takes away from the weapon's power.

The hilt of the blade is made of solid metal and is in the shape of a metal golem's face. There are four large spikes coming out of the golem's head. Two of them come out on either side of the golem's head, and the other two out of where his cheeks would be. Serving as the golem's eyes are two blue gemstones, most likely sapphires.

Lenya twirls the daggers around in the air before sliding them into her waistband. "Now I just need some armor!" she whispers to herself before scanning the floor again.

Meanwhile Von is still outside looking around the grassy plains. When he looks up into the sky, he can just barely see the stars through the smoke from the burning city behind him that is tainting the sky.

"Where are you, Scarlet?" Von mumbles to himself.

Von is staring off into the sky as Pelisus walks up to him and stands next to him. Von looks over to acknowledge Pelisus before looking back at the sky. The two of them stare off into the emptiness above them before Pelisus breaks the silence.

"Are you going to be okay, Von?"

Von nods to Pelisus. "Yeah … I'll be fine. I just need some time to think."

"Think of what?" Pelisus asks Von.

"Where Scarlet is going next," Von says to Pelisus.

"You can't let this eat you alive …" Pelisus says to Von.

"Yeah? And I can't let any more innocent people die because of my psychotic brother," Von says to Pelisus.

Pelisus goes silent and slightly nods to Von, who looks back to the sky. He takes a deep breath in and out, turning back to Von.

"Lenya and I collected a set of armor for you. We stored it inside the inn, next to your bed. When you're done out here, you should come and get some rest," Pelisus says to Von.

Von nods to Pelisus without even turning to look at him. As Pelisus is walking away Von turns around and starts to talk.

"When we do find Scarlet … do you think we will be able to defeat him?" Von asks Pelisus.

"I sure do hope so," Pelisus replies before walking back toward to the inn.

A slight smile comes over Von's face thanks to Pelisus's response. To relieve more stress, Von decides to go for a quick walk around the city. He steps out of the broken gate and walks a bit west, toward the Ochre Plains, before following a path that leads north around the city. Walking on the path, he looks around and enjoys all the different things there are to see.

The grass is growing so tall around the path. Even though he has been in this area before, all Von can remember is the Western Desert and the Misty Woods. The part of him that remembers the tall grass, his hometown of Milem, and everything that happened before the dark elves found him is still gone. Von took in a deep breath with his nose to get a fair smell of the nature around him. As he sucks in the air, a giant smile comes across his face.

The smell of the midnight air and wildlife around him fills his nostrils. He exhales he continues to walk down the path around Ethun. Von can hear the sounds of crickets and locusts in the distance. Each of them is playing its song into the midnight sky. As Von continues down the path, he can hear a unique noise approaching him from the north. At first he is unable to distinguish the sound. But as it draws closer, he is able to make it out to be the pitter patter of horse hooves.

Von unsheathes his sword as he waits to see who is approaching him on horseback. When the horse gets close enough for Von to see, he raises his weapon, ready to strike if it gets too close. On top of the horse sits a hooded man. The robe he is wearing looks to be an old bed sheet pulled over top of him. You can tell that the man's main purpose of the robe was to conceal his identity. Before getting too close to Von, the man rears his horse and stops.

"Don't be alarmed, boy," the man says to Von as he arrives. Von notices that the man has a raspy voice, that of a much older man. "I've only come to talk," the man adds.

"Talk about what? Can't you see we're busy here?" Von asks.

"Yes, I understand. I just have news of your brother, that is all."

"My … my brother? Where is he?" Von asks in a very demanding tone.

"That is not what I am here for. I am here to show you your past, more specifically, the part of it that you want to see," the man says to Von.

"But first, I need you to do something for me. I need you to meet me in Genisus, to the north, two days from now on the far northern dock. Around midnight, meet me there if you wish to learn of your past."

The man rears his horse and turns away from Von. Before Von is able to say anything, the man snaps the reins and rides away. Von is left standing there, staring off into the field to the north as he watches the man ride away. He silently asks himself, "How could this man possibly know about my brother. Who was he?"

Von smiles and makes up his mind about going to Genisus. In order to make it in two days, he is going to need to get a good night's sleep. With this taken into consideration, Von turns around and walks back to the inn in town. Pelisus and Lenya are both sleeping comfortably inside. Von looks around and notices a full set of armor for him that is lying next to a bed. He smiles before placing his swords down onto the ground and crawling under the covers. Von stares at the wall for a few minutes before closing his eyes and drifting off into a deep sleep.

# Chapter 4
# The Port City of Genisus

The next morning, Von wakes up with the sun shining directly on his face. Once awake, he looks around the room. Everyone is still sound asleep. Von rubs his eyes and stretches his arms. The light from the morning sun is seeping into the building through the windows and cracks in the wall from the battle the night before. Von slips into the armor at his bedside, trying to be quiet and not wake anyone up.

Von's armor is solid plate mail. The whole set weighs right around one hundred pounds. What it lacks in mobility it makes up for in defense. At Von's side, he has two large holders for both of his swords. Since they're so unique, however, they fit loosely in the holders. The set of plate mail itself is rather bland. It is just solid metal without a specific design. Across the breastplate there are a few pieces of leather tied to it, presumably for hooking a canteen or something of that matter.

Putting all of his armor on, he sheathes his weapons, walking over to one of the windows in the room. Von bends over and picks up a piece of broken glass, holding it up to see a reflection of himself.

Shockingly, the whole set of plate mail fits Von rather well, aside from the helm, which Von is not wearing. It looks almost as if it was designed for a half-elf of his size. Von tosses the mirror down on the ground and walks outside of the inn. It is almost impossible for Von to sneak through the inn with how much noise the plate mail makes while he walks. Outside he looks around at the destroyed city around him. All of the fires have gone out, and the ground is a little wet from what looks to be rainfall last night.

Continuing to explore, Von walks out the western gate and over to the northern part of the city. Once there, Von stares off at the Plains of Genisus in front of him. The tall grass in the plains is majestically blowing in the wind as the summer sun rises in the sky and melts the water off of them from the night before. Von stares off at the plains to the north, and Lenya and Pelisus walk out of the city and over to him.

Lenya smiles before asking, "You ready for the big journey today?"

Von nods. "As ready as I will ever be."

Von turns to look at Lenya. He notices that she got rid of her slave clothes from Cathunder. Now she has on a fancy leather set of armor. The whole set is pure black, giving her the maximum amount of secrecy in the night. The legs and tunic are multiple pieces of leather bolted together. It almost could pass as scale armor with how they designed the leather. Each "scale" on her tunic is about four inches long and three inches wide.

It continues this pattern all the way down until it reaches her shoes, which are still the same. The shoulders of her leather armor are in the shape of a bird's head. The bird's head fits in well with the armor, but the beak sticks out almost like a spike. As for the sleeves, the suit of armor doesn't offer any protection. Lenya went for maximum mobility over maximum protection.

Von smiles to Lenya as they start the long walk north. Pelisus follows closely right behind Von, with Lenya behind him. Von does his best to follow the hoof prints left by the man's horse from the night before. But after he comes over the large hill to the north of Ethun, he loses them. From on top of the hill, Von is able to see almost all of the Plains of Genisus. There is an occasional tree scattered throughout the plains and even an old broken down fence here and there.

From the top of the hill, Von is able to see the Ochre Plains to the west. A large and long fence separates the golden plains that are Ochre and the green plains that are Genisus. Von walks down from the hill and continues north toward Genisus. The grass is waist tall, which makes traveling through it exceptionally difficult, as their feet and armor are constantly getting caught in it.

Occasionally they will run into a path that is commonly used by the deer of the area. The paths are so commonly traversed that the grass is pushed down to the ground. This makes travel much easier. Generally the paths loop around in a direction they don't want to go, however, forcing them to leave them shortly after they find them.

They walk across the plains until about midday, when they find a large oak tree to take a quick break under. The tree sits in the middle of the field and is roughly one hundred feet tall. Based on the height of the tree, it is probably well over two hundred years old. The branches and leaves of the tree completely block out the sun above everyone, allowing them to feel the cool summer breeze that flows underneath the tree.

Five minutes pass, and Von stands up and nods to everyone, letting them know that it is time to continue their journey. Walking through the tall grass is rough for everyone, but exceptionally rough for Von with his new plate mail armor, weighing in at over one hundred pounds, and the amount of heat it absorbs from the sun. The walk for Von is dangerous as he battles exhaustion and heat stroke throughout the day, but still he pushes on.

A few miles north of the tree, Von spots some smoke billowing up into the air. He doesn't pay much attention to it until he gets closer and sees that there is a small camp built up ahead. There are three leopard skin tents at this camp with a large fire in the middle. It looks like anyone who lived there is out for the time being. Lenya and Pelisus creep up next to Von and stare over to the camp as well, curious of what it is for.

"What do you guys think?" Von asks Pelisus and Lenya.

"It is probably a camp of bandits … That is my guess," Pelisus says.

"Yeah, I agree with Pelisus on this one," Lenya says.

"We should probably avoid the camp; we don't want to have any unnecessary bloodshed," Pelisus says to Von.

"Yeah, let's sneak around the left-hand side through the grass. Keep your heads down, and don't try and peek over there. Follow my lead and they shouldn't see us," Von says to Pelisus and Lenya.

The two of them nod and follow Von's example in leaning down and walking forward. Their backs are about equal level with the grass around them. If someone was just glancing over at them, he would have never seen them. But if someone heard something and actually paid attention, he'd be able to see them quite easily. With the three of them trying to sneak past the camp, travel was much harder. Not only did they have to move at half the speed, but more of their limbs were susceptible to getting tangled in the weeds.

Von's plate mail was constantly getting tangled in the weeds around him. Usually he was able to just rip the grass out of the ground when it got tangled up in his armor, but sometimes he was forced to stop and pull it out manually. This was a huge inconvenience for him since it happened at least every minute or two. As they slowly sneaked by the bandit camp, they could hear commotion from inside of one of the tents. It sounded as if two people were arguing over something.

Hearing the commotion the people burst out of the tent and into the center of the camp. It was a younger couple who was arguing. Von paid no attention to what the argument was about and focused on just sneaking by the bandit camp. When he was crawling through the deep grass, the sun hit Von's armor just right and reflected some light back to one of the bandits arguing in the camp. Everyone's heart dropped down into the pit of their stomachs when they heard the bandit talk.

"Hey, did you see that? Over there in that grass," the bandit said to his girlfriend.

She shakes her head side to side. "No, what are you talking about? You better not be trying to change the subject on me again!" the girl yells at him.

Von, Lenya, and Pelisus stop and watch into the camp, waiting to see what the bandits will do. After the girl's sarcastic response, they start to argue again, paying less attention to the reflection they saw over in the grass a few seconds ago. Von motions Lenya and Pelisus to follow him again before starting to continue north. Now they are a little bit more than halfway by the camp. They have a few more tents to pass and then there is a hill they need to go over. After that, they are in the clear.

As Von is sneaking past the couple arguing, the man pauses and stares off into the grass again. "No, seriously, I can see something over there moving around," the man says to the girl. She turns around and looks over at the grass and nods to him, noticing something too.

"We have intruders!" the man yells out to the rest of the bandits at the camp.

Von enters a panicked state as he tries to decide if running would be a good idea or if he should stay and fight. When he looks over, he notices at least ten bandits coming out of their tents who are ready to kill whatever it was in the bushes.

"Was it an animal?" one of the bandits asks another.

"No, light reflected off of it, so it had to be a sword or armor or something shiny," the bandit replies.

"Oooh, I like shiny things," another bandit says.

Von takes in a deep breath before standing up and turning to face the bandits. Lenya grabs a hold of his arm before he fully stands up and tries to stop him but is unsuccessful. As Von stands up, all the bandits see him and raise their weapons, ready to fight.

"See! I told you that I saw something!" the bandit who originally spotted them exclaims.

"Yeah, now is not the time to get excited because you were right for the first time in your life," another bandit adds.

"Are you two going to shut up so I can talk?" Von asks the two bandits.

Everyone at the camp goes quiet and stares at Von, not sure what he has in mind. Von smirks a bit and clears his throat before starting to speak again.

"All right, a few friends and I are trying to pass and get to Genisus. We stumbled across this bandit camp and decided to sneak by, figuring we wouldn't disturb you and start this large speech about shiny loot and stupid stuff like that," Von says. "So, if you let me and my friends pass, there will be no trouble," Von adds before waiting for their response.

"Ha ha ha, do you honestly think we're going to let you pass?" one bandit asks Von before stepping forward.

"No. To be honest, I figured I would have to kill all of you," Von says in a perfectly calm, serious voice.

"Ha, ha, ha. We met ourselves a comedian, lad. Do you honestly believe that you can kill all of us?" the same bandit who stepped forward asks.

"Don't do it, Von …" Lenya whispers up to Von.

"Believe? Do you understand what I've just done to get to where I am standing now? I've gone into Cathunder and killed over one hundred gnolls, Do *you* honestly believe a pack of bandits scares me?" Von says out loud.

He pulls out both of his swords and holds them where everyone can see them. A large smile comes over Von's face before he cracks his neck and stares forward.

"If you think you can kill me, let's see you try," Von says to the bandits.

"What do you think, boys? Should we rob this man for all that he is worth?" the bandit who looks to be their leader says.

"Yeah, let's do it," all the other bandits respond.

Von steps forward out of the grass and onto the dirt surrounding the bandit camp. He flicks his hair back as an even larger smile crosses his face. Just as he is about to charge into the bandit camp, Lenya jolts up out of the grass from behind him.

"Von! No!" she yells out.

"Oh look, he has a pretty girl with him who is concerned for his safety," a bandit in the crowd says.

"There is no reason to harm all these people, Von; they're just trying to survive," Lenya says to Von sincerely.

"Hey, Von, why don't you tell your pretty girlfriend that she is going to become the camp's new whore when we kill you?" the leader of the bandits says.

A look of anger crosses Lenya's face as she looks to Von and says, "Never mind. Fuck them up."

"Heh," Von says before twirling his swords around and charging into the camp. The first bandit to go down is their leader. Von runs full speed into him and shoves both of his swords through his chest before tearing them out his sides. Intestines and blood shoot everywhere all over the ground, causing the faint of heart to gag.

As everyone is still in shock over what happened to their leader, Von decapitates another bandit and cuts through the third one like he was paper. The remaining seven bandits ready their weapons and watch Von closely. Each of the bandits now knows that they have greatly underestimated his abilities as a warrior. The bandits rush forward toward Von, with their swords swinging in the air.

Von blocks all of their attacks but one, which he can hear bang the side of his plate mail armor. Luckily the blade wasn't sharp enough, and his armor is made for such a hit. Von breaks free from the middle of their attacks and sticks both of his weapons out before spinning around violently. One of the bandits was caught in the whirlwind and torn apart by it.

With only six left, Von throws his swords into two of the bandits standing around him. The swords impale the bandits' bodies and cause them to fall to the ground immediately. With four bandits left, Von is standing in the middle of the camp without a weapon. The bandits chuckle and think it is going to be an easy win, but they are wrong.

Two bandits charge Von. He grabs the arm of one of them and breaks it at the elbow. The bandit's hand still grips the sword tightly, even though it is broken. Von takes advantage of this and bends the arm back, causing the person to stab himself in the face with his own weapon. As Von bends the arm back, he kicks forward to knock the other bandit charging him back.

The bandit comes forward again Von throws a punch and connects with the bandit's face. The bandit stumbles backward and is quickly overwhelmed by a few more violent blows to the chest. The two remaining bandits charge Von from the back. One of them jumps onto his back and tries to cut his neck open with their dagger. Von thrusts his head backward and makes contact with the bandit's nose, causing each of the bones in it to break and blood to gush out.

After that bandit is taken care of, Von spins around and catches the other one's arm mid swing. He twists the bandit's hand until he releases his grip of the sword. With the bandit now disarmed and Von holding him in a position he can't break free of, he proceeds to continuously punch the bandit's face in. Each strike to the bandit's face draws blood, more than the last one. After a few punches from Von, the bandit goes limp and falls to the ground, unconscious.

Von grabs the sword off the ground and shoves it into the chest of one of the remaining bandits. With that now done, he casually walks over to his two swords and pulls them each out of the bodies. Von cleans his weapons off on the dead bandit's clothing before putting them back into their holders.

With the fight now over, Lenya and Pelisus walk into the camp and look around at the destruction Von has caused. Eight of the ten bandits are dead, and two of them are unconscious. Von takes a drink from their water source in the center of the camp and looks inside each of the tents for any useful supplies. Von walks up to the last tent in the camp, and he can hear a slight whimper from inside. He pulls out his sword before opening the tent to see who is inside.

It is a younger girl with black hair. She is naked, with ropes tied around each part of her body and a blindfold pulled over her eyes. Von steps into the tent and pulls her blindfold off to reveal her dark green eyes. She is quivering while looking at Von. She shows serious signs of starvation and dehydration. The young girl's eyes leave a permanent scar on Von's heart. They're almost completely glazed over as they stare at Von. She is unable to speak because of her gag, but she is telling Von with her eyes, "Please don't hurt me."

"Come on, I'll help you out," Von says before starting to cut all of the ropes.

As Von puts the sword near the girl, she shakes and groans. Von assures her that it is okay and he isn't here to harm her. She nods to Von, letting him know that it is okay to continue. While Von is cutting the ropes, Lenya walks up to the tent and looks inside. When she sees the girl, she gasps, unable to believe that someone was put through something that horrible. Lenya decides to run around the bandit camp and collects a pair of clothes for her to wear. Once Von frees her, Lenya walks back with the pair of clothes and hands it to her.

"Put these on. We will wait outside for you," Lenya says to the young girl.

The young girl nods to Lenya, still unable to speak. Von steps outside with Lenya and Pelisus while the young girl gets changed inside the tent. A few minutes go by before she steps out and smiles to the three of them. Von looks at the side of her head and notices her longer ears, that of an elf. She looks to be very young, probably around the age of sixteen or younger.

"What's your name?" Von asks the little girl.

"I'm … I'm Luna," she says in a very quiet voice.

Von lightly grabs her by the arm and escorts her over to the well in the center of the camp. He points to it before smiling and saying, "Take a drink. I'm sure you need one." Luna smiles to Von and starts to drink from the well. Luna takes a long, much-needed drink from the well, and Von walks back to Lenya. Lenya has a horrified look on her face as she watches the young girl.

"I can't believe they did this to her," she says to Von.

"I know … We need to take her to Genisus where she can get some real help," Von says to Lenya.

"It is still at least a day and a half walk from here. It will take even longer since she will need to stop a lot," Pelisus adds.

Von looks away and remembers the man on the horse. He told him that he needed to be in Genisus two nights from then and meet him on the far northern dock to talk. Von swallows hard before turning back to Lenya and Pelisus.

"We should take some of the food here and make sure we keep her well fed. We need to make it to Genisus as soon as possible to get her the help that she needs," Von says to everyone.

Luna finishes drinking out of the well and turns around to face Von and the others. Everyone continues to talk until they realize that Luna is done drinking, at which point they devote their attention to her.

"Thank you for saving me. But there is no need for you to worry too much about my safety," Luna says to them in an almost fully recovered voice.

"Why is that?" Von asks curiously.

"I'm an elven sorceress; I think I may be of help to you guys," Luna says to Von. "After all, you saved me. I owe you my life," Luna says to Von while blushing a bit.

"How old are you, Luna?" Lenya asks.

"I'm seventeen, but much older in elf years," she says with a bright smile.

Lenya continues to talk to Luna as Von searches the camp for any food they can take with them. A few minutes pass, and all Von can find is a few bags of breadcrumbs from the corpses of the bandits. He walks over to Luna and hands them to her. "Here. It's not much, but it is better than nothing," he says to her with a smile.

"Thank you," Luna replies.

Luna sits down and starts to eat the bread crumbs that Von handed to her. In between shoving food into her mouth, she looks up and asks, "So, you guys never introduced yourselves."

Von smiles and says, "Well, my name is Von. This is Lenya, and this is my friend Pelisus."

"Von … That is such a cute name!" Luna says with a smile before blushing again.

Luna looks over to Pelisus and asks, "You're a dark elf. Why are you traveling with the others?"

"I helped Von escape from Terrova. My king was going to execute him," Pelisus says to Luna.

"But why?" Luna asks Pelisus.

"My king is a very corrupt—" Pelisus starts to say but Luna interrupts him.

"No, I mean why did you choose to save him?"

"I saw good in Von, and I haven't been proven wrong thus far about the good I've seen in him," Pelisus says to Luna.

Luna finishes eating the bread that Von gave her before standing up and patting her belly. A large smile comes across her face as she looks at the three of them standing in front of her. "Okay! Where to now?" she asks.

"We are on our way to Genisus. You are more than welcome to join us," Von says to the young girl.

She smiles and tosses her hair before nodding to Von. "Okay, I'll go!" she almost yells out in excitement. Lenya rolls her eyes and follows Von as he starts to walk north again. Luna quickly catches up and walks next to Von through the grass. Von chuckles a bit to himself, being unable to help noticing her crush.

The four of them continue on their journey to the north. Von occasionally asks Luna if she needs to stop for a break, but she presses on. She is young and full of energy, and she also wants to impress Von. As the day continues on and the sun starts to come down from its peak in the sky, the cool winds that blow across the field became much more refreshing.

Without the sun baking the four of them, the walk through the plains was much easier. Any heat that the sun did put off was quickly swept away by the cool breezes. With the sun almost fully set in the sky, Von notices a large river up ahead. He pointed it out to everyone and declared that was where they should make camp for the night. They walked over to the river and set down their belongings next to the river bed.

A good ten feet on both sides of the river didn't have the long grass they've been walking through all day, making it perfect for a camp. However, with no trees around or any wood, they will be unable to get a campfire going. As everyone relaxed behind him, Von walked over to the side of the river and sat down. He stared off at the horizon in front of him and marveled in its beauty.

Watching the sun set over the Ochre Plains to the west was just amazing. The golden fields of the Ochre Plains blended perfectly with the reds, oranges, and pinks of the setting sun. Von stared off into the distance for what seemed like forever well after the sun set, leaving the deep blues of the heavens and thousands of friendly starts pinpointing the night sky. The reflection of the moon was visible in the river right in front of where Von was sitting. The bright glow of the moon reflecting off of the water of the river brought a smile to Von's face. He stared at the reflection for close to an hour. The whole time he thought of Lenya, as the moon's beauty almost matched hers.

When it was finally time to go to sleep for the night, Von stood up and walked back to where everyone else was sleeping. He laid down next to all of them and gave the moon one last look before closing his eyes and falling asleep.

✦       ✦       ✦       ✦

The next morning Von is awoken by the warm rays of the sun beating against his face. When he goes to open his eyes, he is almost immediately blinded by the sun beaming down onto him, forcing him to put his hand over his forehead to act like a visor. Upon looking around, Von notices that everyone is asleep aside from Luna, who is sitting by the side of the river a bit downstream.

Von stretches his arms, pushing himself onto his feet and walking down stream toward Luna. When Von gets close enough, Luna hears him and turns around to look back at him. A slight smile comes across her face before she turns back toward the river. Von walks up to the side of Luna and takes a seat on a large rock to her right. Luna doesn't turn to look at him; instead, she focuses on the river in front of her.

"What's wrong?" Von asks her.

Luna turns her head slightly to look at Von. A small smile comes across her face before she ignores him and turns back toward the river.

"It's okay, Luna, you can talk to me," Von says to her in a very sympathetic voice.

Even with Von's reassurance, Luna still doesn't budge. This time she doesn't even make the slightest effort to even turn and look at Von.

"Luna, the bandit camp is all behind you now. You're safe with us," Von says to Luna.

Luna shakes her head side to side. She starts slow at first but quickly picks up the speed until she speaks, "I'm not worried about that. They raided my town and took everyone. I think I was the only survivor ..."

"Where is your town located?" Von asks her.

"Just northwest of here, it is a small town called Milem," she replies.

"Mi ... Milem?" Von asks her.

"Yeah, it was burned to the ground a long time ago, but my people found it and rebuilt it."

"A long time ago?" Von asks Luna.

"Yeah, they said based on the decay of the wood at least over one hundred years."

"One hundred years ago …" Von mumbles very faintly.

"What did you say?" Luna asks Von.

"Uhm, nothing, nothing," Von quickly replies.

"Did the bandits … Did they burn Milem again?" Von asks Luna.

"No. They just took everybody as far as I can remember," Luna replies.

"How far of a walk is it from here?" Von asks.

"It is probably a few hours, why?" Luna asks Von.

"Let's go," Von says to Luna before standing up and turning around.

"All right, everyone up! We're heading out!" Von yells out to everyone still sleeping. "Pelisus, Lenya, get up come on, let's go!"

Pelisus and Lenya both roll over and turn to look at Von, confused by what is going on. Von looks at them and motions for them to stand up and get ready. They both sit up and rub their faces, trying to shake off the previous night. Von gives them a few minutes to wake up before telling everyone where he is heading. When Lenya hears the news, her eyes light up, anxious to see what her home town is like now.

When everyone is ready, Von leads them northwest, over the river and toward where Luna says Milem is. Walking through the plains of Genisus was much different in the morning. The summer sun has yet to bake off the morning dew from the grass, making the walk a bit slippery. Aside from the slippery nature of the wet grass, others aside from Von have to deal with wet clothes from all the accumulated moisture.

The fresh smell of the morning air fills everyone's nostrils. It was almost as if when night ended all of the plants and trees awakened and started to release their specific scent into the air. As the wind blew, it would pick up all of the scents and travel them across the plain, gathering even more. The smell consisted of dozens of different flowers combined with the smell of freshly cut grass. With all the different smells filling the air it would be impossible to name all of the flowers involved.

As the four of them continue their journey through the plains, Von spots a large smoke cloud in the distance. It is billowing up into the sky from what seems like a large forest nearby. When Luna comes over top of the hill and sees the smoke cloud, she gasps and covers her mouth.

"That's Milem," she says out loud.

"We've got to hurry!" Von replies.

Von takes off through the tall grass, running as fast as possible through it toward the woods. It takes him ten minutes to reach the tree line of the forest. Shockingly, running through the woods is much easier than running across the plain. There isn't a lot of grass to slow him down now, only a few logs that he can easily jump over. As he gets closer to the city of Milem, Von notices that smoke is filling up the woods around him. There is a light haze throughout the woods, making it difficult to see and even more difficult to breathe.

Von reaches a large opening in the woods and looks up into the sky again to see the smoke. "Looks like only another quarter mile," Von says. He turns around and looks behind him to see Lenya, Pelisus, and Luna trying to keep up with him. Von waits a few more seconds for them to catch up before darting in the direction of Milem.

As Von gets closer to the burning town, the smoke throughout the woods only becomes worse. It stinks of burning wood, metal, and flesh. Running through the woods, Von finally finds a broken in path, big enough for a horse buggy, leading into the town. He turns up the path and follows it straight into the center of Milem. The path has two large crevices in it, which the wheels have caused from the multiple carts that come in and out of the city.

The center of the path is perfectly intact, though. Von tries to keep to the center of the path to prevent breaking an ankle or getting tangled in a vine in the small crevices around it. As Von reaches the end of the path, he stops and stares at Milem in front of him. Every building of the city is on fire, and there is absolutely no sign of life. Von falls to his knees as a tear rolls down his cheek. A large white hue forms around each of the buildings in the city before Von blacks out.

❖       ❖       ❖       ❖

"Von, Von, wake up!" An unfamiliar voice says to him.

"Come, on sweetie! Your brother is coming back to visit today," the voice says again.

Von opens his eyes and looks up at the lady. She is much older, with dirty blonde hair and cobalt blue eyes. Von doesn't remember ever seeing this women, but the first thought that popped into his mind was mother.

"I've prepared breakfast for you. Get dressed and hurry down to eat. Your brother will be here soon!" the woman says to Von before walking away.

Von quickly gets out of bed and throws on a pair of tattered clothes his mom left out for him before going downstairs. When he reaches the first floor of his house, he can smell a fresh breakfast consisting of eggs, bacon, and sausage, all specifically prepared for him. Von bypasses the breakfast on the table and walks outside.

The town is in perfect condition. Nothing is destroyed; nothing is burned. All of the townsfolk are still alive and have no idea what is about to happen. Von takes in a deep breath before going back inside to see his mother. He looks all throughout the house but can't find her.

"Mom! We need to get out of here! Something bad is about to happen!" Von calls out throughout the house.

He doesn't get a single response from his mother. Without hearing anything from his mother, Von frantically runs around the house and checks every room, looking for his mother. The whole house is clear. There is no sign of his mother anywhere. Von sits down at the bottom of the stairs and places his head into the palms of his hands. He lets out a long sigh before a voice echoes throughout his head.

"You can't change the past, Von … No matter how much you want to."

"Scarlet? Where are you!" Von stands up and calls out after hearing the voice.

"Guess."

Von looks around the house for his brother before remembering that Scarlet arrived on a horse from outside. Von rushes outside he sees Scarlet standing over the woman from his last vision. Her throat has already been cut open, and she is lying lifeless on the ground.

Von gasps before running over to her and crouching down to see if she is still alive. She isn't.

Scarlet walks over to the center of the town and raises his arms up into the sky before saying, "Nieuro Ferro." Just like before, large fireballs begin to rain down from the sky, killing everyone they come into contact with and setting almost every building on fire. Von stands up and grabs a sword off the ground before running full speed toward his brother.

His brother is standing next to the well, laughing manically as the fire destroys the town around him. Von shoves the sword straight through Scarlet's abdomen and through his backside. With the sword is inside of Scarlet, Von twists it violently before letting go. Scarlet slaps Von, knocking him back before collapsing to the ground. Scarlet grabs the sword with both of his hands and slowly pulls it out from his body. He drops the sword to the ground and screams in agony at Von. Out of anger, Scarlet reaches for his sword and walks over to his brother, who is on the ground.

Von uses his feet to try and crawl away from his brother but can't. Standing over his brother Scarlet raises the sword in the air and thrusts it down through Von, who is on the ground. Scarlet has one hand gingerly placed over his wound while the other is holding onto the grip of the sword sticking out of Von. Scarlet leaves the sword in place before walking away from his brother. Von brings one hand up to the sword and feels it. The metal of the blade is cold, like Von's body. Every time Von breathes, his chest is pushed further up and down the blade, making breathing almost unbearable.

A few more seconds go by before everything turns black. Among the blackness Von can hear a voice, high pitched and squeaky.

"Well, well, what do we have here? Oh, another survivor? Well let's get you back to my lab and quickly, yes? I may just be able to save you and that other lad, the one with the red hair. Yes, yes, I will save you …"

◈　　◈　　◈　　◈

"Von … Von, wake up!" Lenya says as Von slowly starts to open his eyes.

As Von regains consciousness he realizes that he is lying in Lenya's arms. Standing up behind Lenya are both Luna and Pelisus, who are looking down at Von, making sure he is okay.

"What happened, Von?" Lenya asks.

"I saw … I saw what happened here," Von replies. "My brother was casting a spell to burn down the whole town. I stopped him by shoving a sword right through him. But it didn't kill him … He used his sword to pin me to the ground and then left me there. I remember closing my eyes with nothing but death on my mind and then I heard some voice. I never heard before. Someone saying they were going to take me to some sort of lab," Von says.

Von shakes his head, trying to stand up. When trying to stand up, he stumbles a bit, falling back into Lenya's hands.

"Are you okay to walk?" Lenya asks Von in a concerned voice.

"I just need a few minutes," Von replies.

Lenya nods, looking up at the burning village in front of them. The fires have almost consumed all of the houses now, leaving the village just like it was many years ago. As the houses continue to burn, Von slowly regains consciousness. Von is eventually able to stand up and stumble around a bit. Once he regains the ability to walk, Von walks around the burning village. He stops in front of his house and looks at it.

The roof is almost fully caved in, and flames have already fully engulfed the house. Large structural beams that once held the house up have now fallen down and took a great portion of the house with them. Von watches as his childhood home falls to the ground before his eyes. Von is watching the destruction. Lenya walks up behind him and places her arm around his shoulder.

"There is nothing you could have done, Von," Lenya says to him.

"I'm going to find Scarlet … And kill him to end this …" Von says.

"Von …" Lenya starts to say as Von turns his back and walks away.

Von doesn't speak a word as he follows the path north through Milem. Lenya motions to Pelisus and Luna so they know that it is ok to follow Von. The three of them follow Von down the path in the woods, each making sure to keep their distance and let him cool off as well as take everything in. Von mumbles to himself while walking through the woods.

"So ... I died ... And was brought back ... Am I .... Am I a monster?" Von asks himself. "Was I ever human?" Von adds.

"Lab, the man said that saved me said lab, why a lab? What kind of experiments was I used for?"

Von continually questions himself while walking away from the burning village of Milem. The further Von gets away from the burning village, the less smoke that fills the woods. All of the wildlife and trees around the path leading north are becoming more visible. With the air clearing up, it is also becoming much easier to breathe. A slight feeling of lightheadedness comes over Von as he finally gets his first few breaths of fresh air in awhile.

Lenya, Pelisus, and Luna all follow Von up the path. Each of them is careful enough to not make noise or even let Von know that he is being followed. Von is walking at a hastened pace. His mind is focused on his last vision and getting to Genisus. In Genisus, he will learn what the cloaked man has to say; maybe he will even be able to answer the questions from the vision in Milem.

The path continuously loops and bends through the woods, making it difficult to travel in a set direction. Each side of the path leading north through the forest looks the same. Dozens of trees cover the landscape, with little bushes in between each one. Occasionally while walking through the woods, the four of them would alert a deer in the distance. Usually they wouldn't see the deer, but the pitter patter of its feet could be heard in the distance as it ran from them.

Aside from the occasional deer, the woods were silent. The large fire burning in Milem sent all of the animals in the woods running for cover. None of them want to be caught in the blaze. At this point, the smoke in the woods is no longer visible. The only trace left of the burning town of Milem is when the wind blows. It carries the faintest smell of ember and ash over to Von and up into his nostrils.

The four of them walk for another two hours before finally reaching the tree line to the north. In almost a straight line the trees just stop and the Genisus Plains start again. Tall grass fills the fields in front of them as they step out of the thick, treelike wilderness. Walking through the tall grass this time around was much harder than Von remembered.

The grass is constantly getting stuck in between the creases of his plate mail. Every time Von lifts a knee, grass finds its way inside and gets caught when he extends his leg again. The others following Von don't have as hard of a problem as he does, though. Since Pelisus is wearing a robe and others leather, it is almost impossible for grass to get stuck in their armor.

After twenty minutes of Von fighting his way through the tall grass, he decides to take out one of his swords to slice his way through. The idea works great at first, but as time goes on, his arm becomes more and more tired. Eventually Von is forced to switch to his other arm to prevent wearing his right one out too much. As they walk through the field, Von switches back and forth between arms, trying to make sure that he doesn't use one too much more than the other in case something unexpected attacks.

An hour passes of them walking through the field before coming up to a very large hill. The hill is very steep and stands out among the other hills across the plains. There are dozens of stones spread out all over the hill. Some of them are large boulders that you can see through the tall grass and some are small rocks that are almost invisible unless you are right on top of them. The tall grass that fills the Genisus Plains also started to become shorter and shorter as they progressed up the hill.

At the top of the hill, far to the north, was the port city of Genisus. The city itself was still very far away, and the hill they were standing on only provided them with a bird's-eye view. Surrounding the city was a thick wall made of solid stone to protect from outside attackers. On the northern side of the city was the Banished Sea, where many ships go for fishing adventures and never return. There were a few large boats docked at Genisus, which was normal for this time of the year.

The fishing was good, and since it wasn't a rainy season, the waters were calm. The hill that the four of them are standing on is still a few miles south of Genisus. And from the looks of it, navigating back down toward Genisus will be a problem. The northern side of the hill leading down toward Genisus is a very steep decline that is littered with rocks and boulders. Von paces back and forth along the hillside looking for the safest way down but comes up short many times.

Von lets out a reluctant sigh before convincing himself that there is no way down the hill and the only option is to go around. With this decision, Von starts off to the west, where the hill slowly and gradually approaches the ground. While walking to the west, he notices a rope that is tied off to a rock nearby. The rope is so old and tattered that it almost perfectly blends in with the dirt on the ground, which is why Von missed it the first time.

He bends over and grabs the rope before giving it a few tough tugs. The rope shows no signs of breaking and looks like it is tied off well enough to the rock to support everyone's weight. Checking the durability of the rope, Von turns around and looks down the hill to see its path. It weaves in and out between giant boulders that are along the hillside but goes down to the ground below safely.

Von turns to everyone else and nods. "I'll take point. You guys follow me. Be careful, I don't know how much weight this rope can hold, so don't pull too hard on it or put a lot of strain on it."

Everyone nods to Von as he starts down the rope. Von grips the rope with both of his hands and walks backward down the hillside. His head is hanging over his right shoulder so he is able to see where he is going to avoid tripping or falling. Once Von is quarter of the way down the hill, Pelisus grabs a hold of the rope and starts down too. He follows in Von's exact footsteps, figuring Von knows what he is doing, so why change it. Once Pelisus is a quarter of the way down, Lenya follows him and eventually Luna.

The hillside isn't as hard to navigate as Von originally thought. It is steep but with the addition of the rope to help keep his balance, it is no problem at all. When Von is almost to the bottom, he hears a yell from up top. When he turns to look in front of him, he sees Luna lying down, face first on the ground. Behind her is a decent-size rock bouncing down the hill, ready to take out anyone in its way.

Lenya is the first one that had to dodge the rock, which she does easily. As it approaches her she runs up the side of a nearby rock and back flips off of it. When she lands on the ground, the rock is already well past her and on its way to Pelisus. As the rock gets closer to Pelisus, he lets go of the rope with one hand and points it at the rock.

A large tidal wave of energy came out of Pelisus's hand as he submerges the rock back into the ground. As he stops the rock dead in its tracks, a slight smile comes over his face. Everyone faintly chuckles at Pelisus's methods before continuing back down the side of the hill. When Von reaches the bottom, he turns around and looks up at the others. Each of them is still slowly making his or her way down the side of the hill.

While Von waits for the others, he decides to do a quick once-over of the area around him. At first glance, he notices that the grass is much shorter on this side of the hill. Instead of coming up past his waist, it only comes up to his kneecaps. It will still be a moderate inconvenience to walk through but nothing like before. Now that Von is down off the side of the hill, Genisus is no longer in view. They will have to walk a few more miles north and cross over top a few more hills in order to see Genisus again.

With everyone is down off the side of the hill, Von starts off again to the north. With the much smaller grass and numerous trees throughout the area, it is hard to believe he is still in the Genisus Plains. Walking through the plains, they pass the occasional deer that is grazing or a rabbit looking for some food. Even though it was so long ago when Von was in Genisus, he can remember being told about the dangers of the plains: the bandits that were exiled from Genisus litter the plains, the wild boars that graze on the lush grasses, and giant grass snakes, which have a deadly toxin.

Although Von is aware of all of these dangerous things, none of them worry him. The bandits and boars he could see coming, and the grass snakes couldn't bite through his plate mail armor even if they tried. Even if one of the snakes did get lucky enough to bite someone, Pelisus and Luna are around, who could most certainly cure any poisons or diseases.

As they come over top of the first of three hills to the north, they are able to get another glimpse of Genisus. At the very peak of the hill they are able to see the outer walls of Genisus. The guards that are patrolling the top of the walls look like specks in the distance. Going over the peak of the hill causes Genisus to fall out of sight again. On their way to the next hill, Pelisus clears his throat as he gets ready to say something important.

"So, we've yet to cross the bridge and I thought that I am a dark elf and there is no way they will let me into Genisus."

Von slows down his pace and scratches the top of his head before turning around to Pelisus.

"Hmm … Good point. I haven't thought of that. Couldn't we sneak you inside?" Von asks.

"There are too many guards. I already checked," Pelisus replies.

"What about an illusion?" Luna asks Pelisus.

"An illusion … Luna may be on to something here. I could do something like that, although, I'd need someone's characteristics to mimic," Pelisus adds.

"Mimic me," Von adds.

"Mimic you?" Pelisus asks Von questioningly.

"We both grew up in Milem, born as identical twins. Let me do the talking, and we will be okay," Von replies.

"I guess we don't have any other options … Hold up, Von, stand still."

Pelisus runs up to Von as he stops and turns around. Pelisus places his hands on Von's shoulders before closing his eyes. He takes in a long, deep breath as small circles of light arise from the ground. They swirl around Pelisus and Von for almost a minute. A large flash is sent out as the light particles disperse. Luna and Lenya both gasp and look away, not expecting the sudden flash of light. When they look back, Von and Pelisus are staring at each other.

Pelisus now looks exactly like Von; the only way you can tell them apart is Pelisus still has his robe on. As Von opens his eyes he gasps and steps backward. The shock of seeing himself quickly overwhelms him.

"Now this is just weird," Von says.

Pelisus nods, "Think they will buy it?"

"I do," Luna shouts from the back.

"Heh," Von says while smirking.

"We should continue to Genisus. They may not let us in during the night," Von says out loud to everyone.

Everyone nods to Von before following him north again. With Pelisus now in disguise, they don't have to worry about anything when going into Genisus. They travel across the Genisus Plains for the remainder of the afternoon. Just as the sun starts to descend in the sky, they arrive at the front gates of Genisus.

They stop a few dozen feet in front of the gate to the city. Then they wait as the guards mobilize and open them. As the front gate slowly slides open, five guards run out and surround the four of them. All of them have their weapons drawn and shields steadied in front of them, ready to attack if they make the wrong move.

"We don't want any trouble; we just want a place to spend the night," Von says.

The guards ignore Von and start to close in. Von pulls out both of his swords and plants his right leg back, ready to defend himself if the guards try anything. Right after Von does this, a raspy voice can be heard from behind the walls of Genisus.

"Wait!" a man yells out.

All of the guards turn to look back inside of Genisus as a younger man walks around the corner, in his late twenties. He has on a full set of plate mail armor, exactly matching the set Von remembers his brother was given when joining the Royal Guard. The man approaches Von and motions for everyone to lower their weapons. Von complies and lowers his swords, as do the guards in Genisus.

"Who are you?" The man asks Von.

"My name is Von; this is my brother, Pelisus, my wife, Lenya, and our daughter, Luna. We wish to spend the night in Genisus," Von says to the guard. Von figures a lie would be much easier to explain than the whole story.

The man pauses and stares at Von and Pelisus, questioning the two. "You look awfully familiar; do I know you from somewhere?"

"I do not believe so," Von replies.

The man nods to Von before saying, "You may enter Genisus. Please keep your weapons sheathed at all times, and do not cause any trouble."

Von nods to the man and says, "Thank you. May I bother you for one more thing?"

"And what is that?" the man asks.

"Where is the inn? My family and I are quite tired from the walk here, and we are looking for a comfortable bed for the night."

"By the shore to the north, you will find Brenon's Inn. You may spend the night there if you wish," the man says to Von.

"Thank you," Von says with a nod.

Von passes by the man and into Genisus. He smiles, thanking him for being so kind. Once the four of them are inside of Genisus, the guards close the gate behind them and return to their normal positions. Since it is almost nighttime, the streets of Genisus are bustling with all kinds of different people. The poor and rich seem to flow quite well together here and even get along. The fact that Genisus has three different races living here doesn't even seem to matter. There is no discrimination.

The city of Genisus' architecture is a combination of elves and humans. Some buildings you could tell were designed by elves, some humans, and some were even combined styles. The elves' buildings were easy to identify. They all had a large lightning rod-like structure on the roof and were made of stone that was smoothed down as much as possible. The humans' buildings were made more of brick if they were rich and some of wood if they were poor.

The first part of the city that Von walked through was the stores and shops. Dozens and dozens of people were out on the streets buying whatever they needed before the shops close for the night. All of the torches throughout the city were lit. Every building had at least one torch at the side of their doors, and there were torches every ten feet throughout the city. The torches that weren't attached to buildings were impaled in the ground along the path. The torches were at the top of ten-foot poles that were placed equally apart along the path.

Walking through the business part of the city, Von started to stray into the residential part. The buildings were placed further apart in this section of the city, as were the torches. Also, the path changed from stone to dirt. There weren't nearly as many people in the residential part of the city as there was in the business. Occasionally Von would pass a citizen who was on the way back to his or her house. They were all in a big hurry, trying to beat the setting sun in the distance.

Further down the path of the residential part of the city they could see the docks. The boats they saw earlier in the day were gone, and a new set of boats was in. Faintly in the distance they could see people working on the boats, patching up any leaks and unloading the fish they caught during their adventure out at sea. At the end of the dirt path on the right-hand side was a large sign that said "Brenon's Inn."

Von walks over to the building and holds the door open for his three friends before turning inside. It smells like fresh pine needles and looks like it was for mid-class citizens. Von walks over to the counter and smiles at the older elf who is behind it. The elf has long brown hair, almost down to his knees, and long, pointy ears. Von walks up to him, and a large smile comes across his face.

"Do you have four rooms available tonight?" Von asks the elf.

"Actually, you're in luck! We do," the man says.

"How much would all four of them cost?" Von asks.

"Ten gold pieces each, so forty in all. I'll give them to you for thirty-five, though, since you're buying four at once," the man says to Von with a smile.

"Hold on a second please," Von says before turning around to everyone else.

He walks away from the man behind the counter and over to Lenya and the others. They are all grouped around a table in the center of the inn.

"I only have two gold coins, what about you guys?" Von says.

"Three here," Lenya says.

"Two here," Pelisus adds.

"Five!" Luna exclaims.

"Ok, so we have twelve in all ... That is just barely enough for one ..." Von says out loud.

The man behind the counter looks over at Von curiously before turning around and looking at what rooms are available. He runs his hand over all of the keys before finding one that is exceptionally dusty, room twenty-three.

"Excuse me, sir!" the man yells out to Von.

Von turns around and looks at the man before responding, "Yes?"

"Room twenty-three has eight beds. No one ever uses the room because it is rumored to be haunted. But by looking at you folks, it doesn't seem like something that would bother you. I'd be willing to give you the room for twelve gold coins," the man says.

Von smiles to the man behind the counter and nods. "We'll take it."

Von walks over to the man and hands him the twelve gold coins in exchange for the room key. The man points to the staircase leading up stairs and says, "It's the last room on the left at the end of the hall upstairs. Enjoy your night."

Von nods to the man and turns around to walk up the stairs to the second floor. Lenya, Pelisus, and Luna follow right behind him as he leads them to their room. At the end of the hall, on the left-hand side of the second floor of the inn, Von finds the door that the man told him about. The door has cobwebs growing in the corners of it and a thick layer of dust around the bottom. You could tell no one had used the room in a very long time. No one has even entered recently to clean it.

When Von turned the knob on the door and pushed it open, a large creak echoed throughout the hall, and a strong burst of cold air filled the hallway. A low moan could be heard as the door opened, and a musty smell filled the air. Von was the first one to step into the room and take a look around. All of the pictures on the walls were crooked, and a lot of the beds had a thin layer of dust across the top of them.

"Home sweet home ..." Von mumbles.

"I guess you get what you pay for, right?" Pelisus says.

Each of them picks a bed and unburdens themselves with anything they've brought with them. Von takes off his plate mail armor and places it next to his bed before taking a seat. As he sits down, dust shoots up from the bed and into the air. The room is almost instantly filled with the cloud as everyone starts coughing. Pelisus walks over to the windows on the eastern side of the room and opens all of them, letting the dust in the room clear out.

Pelisus opens all of the windows in the room. Everyone grabs their bed sheets and shakes them outside of the window, clearing off the dust that has collected on them over time. When everyone is finished, they lay the sheets back on their beds and lie down. Von lies down on the bed and folds his arms behind his head while staring at the ceiling.

Von waits patiently for everyone to snuggle in their beds and fall asleep. With everyone asleep, he sits up and creeps over to the door leading out into the hallway. Von turns the knob on the door and gently pulls it open, but it still creeks almost as loud as the first time they opened it. Once the door is open, he steps out of the room and closes it behind him very slowly. As he is closing the door, he notices Luna tossing and turning in her bed, possibly from the creak disturbing her.

With the door closed, Von sneaks halfway down the hallway before returning to a normal pace. Everything is quiet inside of the inn, and the only lights are the candles that are hanging off the wall in the hallway. Von takes the stairs leading down to the first floor slowly, trying not to make any noises and wake anyone up inside. Once on the first floor, he looks over to the elf behind the counter and slightly nods.

"Couldn't sleep?" the elf asks Von.

"Nah, I am going to go for a walk to unwind," Von replies.

"All right, I usually lock the doors at two before going to bed. Try to be back before then, okay?" the man asks Von.

"I will," Von says to the man as he opens the front door of the inn.

Von steps outside into the chilly air, and he almost immediately quivers. The winds that blow across the sea are carrying cool air and bringing it directly to Von. He rubs his arms and shivers before walking north toward the docks. Von follows the shoreline until he finds the longest dock. Once he does, he follows it all the way to the end before looking out at the sea.

The waters are calm tonight, and the sky is clear. Von can see each and every one of the stars in the sky, which were lighting the ocean. To the west was a very large lighthouse, which served as the only other light aside from the stars. The ocean went on to the north it eventually collided with the horizon. The stars met the ocean and gave off an unexplainable glow. Von takes in a deep breath of the sea air before sitting down at the end of the dock and looking off into the sea.

Now, all Von is able to do is wait. He held up his end by coming to the docks around midnight; now the older man from the village needs to hold up his. As Von sits at the end of the dock and stares out at the ocean, he listens to the sounds of the waters slapping against the beach behind him. The sound was so soothing and peaceful. It allowed him to almost enter a serene trance as he waited. As he stares out at the ocean, he hears footsteps approaching from the back, followed by a familiar voice.

"Von … is that you?" Lenya says.

Von tilts his head around to look at Lenya before smiling and saying, "Yeah, it's me."

"What are you doing out here at this time of night?" Lenya asks Von.

"I needed a breath of fresh air," Von replies.

"You've been acting strange all day. Are you okay?" Lenya asks.

"Yeah, I am fine," Von says to Lenya.

"Von … Let's not lie to each other right now," says Lenya.

Von tilts his head down toward his lap as Lenya approaches him and sits down next to him. She sits down and he looks over at her before turning his head back toward the ground. She leans into him and throws her arm around his shoulders, pulling him closer to her.

"You know you can tell me anything, right?" Lenya says to him. "When you left Milem, I thought I was never going to see you again. I didn't hear anything about you in Genisus, only things about your brother. What happened to you, Von?"

"I … I don't remember. I don't even remember leaving Milem," Von says as a tear starts to roll down his cheek. "I remember …

Milem being destroyed. I remember … you and me back then. I remember my brother. I remember …"

Von goes silent for a few seconds before slamming his first into the dock and yelling, "Why can't I remember! Why has this happened to me?"

"It is okay, Von. You have me here now. You came back for me. At least you remembered."

Von looks up into the sky after Lenya speaks. The only thought in his mind is that he didn't remember Lenya; Scarlet remembered Lenya. Scarlet is the only one who told Von about Lenya. If it wasn't for Scarlet, Von wouldn't be here right now and Lenya would still be a prisoner. It eats Von up inside, but he bites his lip, not wanting Lenya to know the truth.

"When I was killed in Milem—" Von starts to say but is interrupted by Lenya.

"Von …"

"Please, let me finish," Von says to Lenya. "When I was killed in Milem, I remember someone coming up to me and saying something about bringing me back to a lab. He wanted to save me … I want to know what he did to me. It has to be because of him that I can't remember. I don't even know if I am still me anymore. The person you used to know could be dead, and I could be a puppet, some creation some—"

"Von, please stop," Lenya says, interrupting Von.

Von tilts his head back down toward the ground as more tears start to flow out from his eyes. Lenya pulls him tighter before giving him a kiss on the top of the head.

"You need to get some sleep," Lenya says to Von.

Von nods to Lenya before saying, "I'll come back to the inn in a few minutes. I just need some more time alone."

"All right. Please, Von, be careful," Lenya says to him in a very concerned voice.

Von nods to Lenya. "I will."

Lenya stands up and gently rubs Von's shoulder before walking down the dock and back toward the inn. Von wipes the tears away from his eyes before looking back out toward the ocean. Less than five minutes after Lenya leaves, Von is able to hear footsteps approaching him on the dock again.

"Lenya, I told you I will be back to the inn shortly. Please ... I just need time," Von says.

"Time is something you do not have right now, my child," the mysterious older voice from before says.

Von quickly gathers himself before standing up and turning around to face the man. As he turns around, he realizes that the man is giant, almost eight feet tall. He has on the same robe as before, covering his face to mask his true identity.

"Who are you, and why did you want to meet me here?"

The man doesn't respond. Instead he pulls off the hood over top of his head to reveal his face. He has long gray hair, down to his shoulders, and a full gray beard. Across his forehead and down the right-hand side of his face is a long scar. The man holds his gigantic hand out and places it on Von's right shoulder before speaking.

"My name is Drylor. I am the creator of this world and everything on it," the man says to Von. "I do not expect you to believe me and that is not of my concern. If I was going to lie to you, I would have not shown myself tonight," the old man says to Von.

"I need you to do something for me, Von. Something that will reveal a lot of your past, something that will give you back your memory. Not all of it, but the pieces that you want to remember: your brother, what happened after Milem, why you're capable of much more than a normal human," the man says to Von.

"I need you to defend Genisus tomorrow, from the impending attack."

"What impending attack?" Von asks the man.

"Did you think crippling Cathunder and escaping Terrova would go unremembered? Your brother told them of your presence in Genisus. They are coming to collect your head," the man says to Von.

"A whole city will be destroyed—again—because of me," Von mumbles.

"No. Genisus will not be destroyed. You, Lenya, Pelisus, and Luna will defend it. With your help, you will be able to repel the threat that your brother caused.

"In return, I wish to grant you a gift. After the battle tomorrow, I want you to take a boat far to the north in the Banished Sea. Use this map to find the first of nine artifacts in this world. Upon finding this treasure, you will be granted a gift. You will learn the truth about Milem, your brother, and what happened to you. You will learn why you lost your memory and why you are capable of such power," the man says to Von as he hands him a map. The map is an old piece of paper wrapped up and being held shut by a ring.

"With this gift I ask of you to do something, though. When you touch the artifact, you will be bestowed all of this but given one more simple task. You will learn the location of your brother. You will need to go there, alone, and defeat him. Are you able to do this for me?" the man asks Von.

Von nods to the man. "I don't even know who I am right now. I can't remember anything. I don't even know if I am human … But if it means killing my brother, I will go to the end of the world for you."

"Good. Use this map, find the artifact, and learn the location of your brother. After you've found the artifact, bring it back to me in Genisus. I will meet you at the end of this dock, at the same time, three nights from now. Until then, good-bye, Von."

The older man turns away and pulls the hood over top of his head. Von watches him as he walks down the dock and back into the city of Genisus. Von pulls the ring off of the map and unfolds it before his eyes. On the map is a picture of the world in much detail. Up top, around Genisus there is a circle on the map and a dotted line leading north with an "X" at the end of it.

After looking at the map, Von rolls it back up and slides the ring over it, putting it into his pocket. He takes in one final deep breath of the salty air before walking back toward the inn. Each step Von takes causes the boards on the pier to creak obnoxiously. After years and years of being traversed every day and soaked with salt water, the boards have grown apart from one another. Large gaps have formed and nails have loosened. This makes it so every step causes a board to ever so slightly move and creak.

Von is walking through the residential area of Genisus, and he notices that now almost every house has their lights out. Only a faint glimmer of light can be seen through the windows of some houses. The streets throughout the city are also mostly clear. The only people walking down them are either heading home or guards doing their late-night patrols. As Von arrives back at the inn, he walks inside and slightly nods to the elf behind the counter.

"All done for the night?" the elf asks.

"Yes, I'm done. You can lock up now," Von replies.

The elf smiles and walks over to the front doors of the inn while Von heads up stairs and back to his room. He carefully opens the door to the bedroom, not wanting to wake anyone up if he doesn't need to. Once he gets the door open just enough to fit in, Von wiggles his way through the small gap and closes the door behind himself. Von closes the door, and he tiptoes over to his bed, lying down and looking over at Lenya. Lenya is sound asleep. While waiting for Von, she must have become tired and put her head down to rest her eyes, only to fall asleep. A slight smile comes over Von's face after seeing Lenya so peacefully sleeping. Von turns his head back toward the ceiling and closes his eyes before drifting off into a deep sleep.

# Chapter 5
# The Great Battle

The next morning, everyone in the city is awoken by a loud bell that is being repeatedly struck. Outside of the inn, shouting can be heard from different people. Guards are telling everyone to stay inside and stay calm where as the citizens are yelling at the guards, demanding to know what is going on. As the bell continues to ring, Von sits up out of his bed and looks around the room. Everyone else is just waking up and rubbing their eyes or yawning from the night before.

"What ... what is going on?" Pelisus asks in between yawns.

"The city is going to be attacked today," Von replies.

"Attacked! What? How do you know this?" Lenya asks.

"Long story ... but we are going to need to help defend against the attack. So let's get dressed and see what we can do," Von says.

Everyone nods to Von before standing up and slipping into their armor from the day before. With everyone ready, they grab their weapons and rush out of the inn and into the city of Genisus. The streets are filled with guards trying to convince people to stay inside and people demanding to know what is going on. Von stops next to a guard in the middle of the road who isn't busy and taps him on the shoulder.

"Do you know where they are mobilizing to defend against the attack?" Von asks the guard.

"What attack?" the guard replies, trying to play dumb.

"Don't play stupid with me. We do not have time for this. Tell me who is in charge of the Royal Guard. My friends and I would like to help protect Genisus," Von says to the guard.

"No really, sir, I don't know what you're talking about," the guard replies.

Von throws his hands out toward the guard's neck. He gets a firm grip around his undershirt before twisting it and pulling him close.

"What part of I want to help do you not understand? Tell me who the captain of the Royal Guard is. You need my help in defending the city."

"He … he is at the gates … out front, just please … don't hurt me," the guard replies to Von, starting to shake from the threat.

Von releases his grip from the guard and dashes toward the front gates of the city. The business section of the city is different today. All of the shops are closed, and the area is completely deserted. Von gets closer to the front gates of Genisus. He can hear many people talking. They are all frantically talking over one another, making it almost impossible to figure out what they are saying.

As Von rounds the final corner toward the front gates of Genisus, he is stopped by two guards. Each of the guards is wearing a full set of plate mail armor and holding a long spear. There are five small red ribbons attached to the spears up by the blade, showing what rank the soldiers are.

"Halt!" the soldiers shout out to Von.

"I need to get past. My friends and I are willing to help defend the city against the attack," Von says out loud.

"The attack? How do you know about this?" one of the guards asks.

"Everyone knows about it. You rang the bell this morning," Von replies.

"No! You must be one of them in disguise! You're not going any further, scum," the guard says to Von.

"Heh …" Von mumbles under his breath.

One of the guard lunges forward and shoves his spear straight toward Von. Von grabs it and breaks it in half before pulling out his weapons and going straight for the guard's throat.

"Wait!" someone calls out from behind a building nearby.

Everyone stops what they are doing and pauses as they wait for the man to come out from the alleyway. When the man turns around the corner, Von notices that it is the same one from the day before, the one who let them inside of Genisus.

"Well hello there, Von was it?" the man asks.

Von slightly nods to him without responding.

"My name is Nunnar. I am the captain of the Genisus Royal Guard," Nunnar says to Von as he places his right hand over his chest, showing respect.

Von nods to him. "My friends and I wish to help fight."

"Friends? If I recall correctly yesterday you said they where your family," Nunnar says to Von.

"They—" Von starts to say but is quickly interrupted by Nunnar.

"No need for explanation. I understand. Come with me. We are briefing the troops now, as we will need to be ready by nightfall."

The guards that stopped Von before back away to let him and his friends pass. They follow Nunnar through the city until they reach the crowd surrounding the front gates of Genisus. In the crowd itself there are citizens mixed with guards, and almost 90 percent of them are men. Each of them is armed with some sort of weapon, whether it be a sword, mace, axe, or even a household knife. The crowd forms a crescent moonlike shape around the front doors of the city. Standing right in front of the gates is a much older man with a long gray beard.

He is dressed in royal battle armor, giving the impression that he is the king of Genisus. The man isn't holding a weapon, nor does he have one sheathed at his side. This implies, to Von, that he is just here to give orders.

"Thank you all for coming," the man dressed in royal battle armor says out loud.

"As many of you already know, there is an impending attack on our great city of Genisus. The dark elves, ogres, gnolls, orcs, and goblins are all working together on this one. I've gotten word that they are coming from the back in boats and in the front.

"They are thousands strong, whereas we only have a few hundred. We will need to fight until the very end. We have the advantage. This is our city, and no one knows it better than we do!"

"Our scouts say we have at least five hours to prepare. We need to use it wisely. Grab weapons, armor, and shields, and take your positions!"

After the king finishes his speech, the crowd erupts into applause and cheers. The king bows to everyone a few times before walking away from the front gates of the city. Once the king is out of sight, the crowd starts to disperse. Everyone wants to spend the last few hours before the attack with their families and try to rest a bit beforehand. Von and Pelisus run up to the city's walls and look out at the Genisus Plains.

Faintly in the distance Von and Pelisus can hear the marching of the impending army. The sounds of their armor colliding with their weapons with every step they take echoes across the plains. Von looks over to Pelisus and notices that he has both hands gently pressed against his temples. He waits for Pelisus to break the deep trance before asking him a question.

"What did you see?"

"There are more than a few thousand," Pelisus replies.

"How many do you think?" Von asks.

"Somewhere around fifty thousand, with catapults, rams, archers, and footmen. And if the king was right about them coming in the back as well, then we have even more to worry about," Pelisus says.

"How long do you think we have before they get here?" Von asks.

"They will come over top of that hill in the distance in the hour. From then, maybe another hour tops. It also depends if they stop to start pelting us with cannonballs."

"We should tell Lenya and Luna," Von says to Pelisus.

Pelisus nods to Von as he follows him down off the wall surrounding the city. Von pushes and shoves his way through the crowd until he finds Lenya and Luna. Once he finds them, he notifies them of how close the attack actually is and how they can help defend the city.

"Luna and Pelisus, you will be up front. Help the archers. You guys have range, something Lenya and I don't. Lenya and I will go to the back of the city, by the water and wait for the sea attackers. In the meantime, let's get some food and something to drink. I'm hungry," Von says with a slight chuckle.

Everyone nods to Von, wanting to eat and rest a bit before the battle later today. After all, this could be everyone's last meal. As Von walks through the city and back to the inn, the army approaching from the south is making good progress. As Pelisus predicted, there are much more than a few thousand. The army is so large that all of the Genisus Plains are covered. Almost every two feet there is a gnoll, orc, ogre, dark elf, or some sort of war machinery.

The constant pounding of their footsteps and heavy weight of their machinery completely flattens the grass. This made travel very easy for the troops in the back. Noon was the first hour that you could see the impending army from Genisus. People gathered atop the walls surrounding Genisus and stood in awe as they watched the army approach from the south.

Word was also traveling fast of dark elf boats being spotted just out of sight nearby Genisus. A few of the fisherman who left the port today made it back and had horrific stories to tell about what happened to their crew and boats. As the army encircles Genisus, there is nothing any of them could do but sit around and wait. Von is interested to see how the wait was affecting everyone. Some people sat there quietly and stared at the wall, and some people got drunk to try and quell their emotions.

Von is one of the quiet people. He finds a chair inside the local tavern and sits down. From noon onward, Von just sat there watching people come in and out of the tavern. Almost 90 percent of them came in sober and left shit-faced drunk, knowing that the day won't end well. Around two in the afternoon Pelisus walks into the tavern and over to Von. He leans down and whispers into his ear, "It's time."

Von nods to Pelisus before standing up and following him out of the tavern. Genisus is quiet now. There isn't a single person on the streets aside from Pelisus and Von. As they walk down the road, Von occasionally looks over to one of his sides and into the houses. He could see parents holding their kids tightly as they cowered inside of the house. One house he saw a mother holding her daughter tightly. She kissed her daughter on the side of the head and whispered into her ear, letting her know everything would be okay and Daddy was going to fight the monsters.

After seeing the mother and daughter Von could almost perfectly picture Milem, the past. Scarlet was the monster of his tale, a very powerful one at that. When Von thinks of Scarlet, anger rushes through his veins. He tightly squeezes his fists together and lightly shakes them, wanting nothing more than to use them on Scarlet. Von opens his right hand and watches a small drop of sweat roll down his palm. While watching the tiny bead of sweat roll down his hand, Von says, "I'm going to use this anger on anything that gets in my way today ..."

Pelisus escorts Von over to the wall and points out to the Genisus Plains where the huge army is waiting. Von walks by Pelisus and up the staircase so he can see over the large stone wall. As he reaches the top of the stairs and turns his head to look out into the Genisus Plains, his eyes light up with fear. The green grass of the Genisus Plains is no longer visible, and the only thing able to be seen is the darkened skin colors of the orcs, ogres, and dark elves.

The front line of the enemy force consists of orcs and ogres with heavy armor and a set of rams to bust through the front gates of the city. Behind them is another set of warriors fully equipped to rush in the second they burst down the castle walls. The third line they have is the archers and catapults, both of which are going to be a large problem and significantly deadly today. Von takes in a deep breath before standing up on his tippy-toes and looking back at the harbor.

Out in the harbor, there are a few different boats he is able to see with dark elf flags waving in the wind. Von steps back down and swallows hard before looking out at the army gathered outside of Genisus one more time. There are already up to five thousand of them standing outside, and more are coming over the hills to the south. They look like specks in the distance, but Von can tell there are many more than another few thousand coming here.

When Von turns to look back down into the city, he notices that the guards are now mobilizing by the front gates. Archers are running past Von to get into position before the attack starts. Von stands their almost motionless for close to a minute as he processes everything that is about to happen. Everyone gets into place inside of Genisus and goes silent as they watch the army to the south. The only thing that can be heard is the sounds of the army marching toward Genisus from the south.

Their metal boots smash against the ground in unison and send a shockwave of noise across the plains. Everyone readies themselves and watches the army, waiting to see what their next move will be. As minutes go by, more and more troops arrive at the back lines of the enemies, and even more continue over the hills to the south. Small talk breaks out amongst the troops, and each of them discuss their worry of the fight today.

The small talk continues until the sounds of marching to the south immediately stop. Everyone goes silent as they peer over the city's walls and at the army below. Each of them is standing there motionless watching, waiting to commence their next move. A few minutes of silence pass before a large battle cry echoes out across the army to the south. Each of the enemies throw their arms up into the sky and yell at the top of their lungs. Von closes his eyes as a strong chill runs down his spine.

"Archers, fire!" Von hears shouted by one of the commanders in Genisus.

When Von opens his eyes, he looks up into the sky and sees hundreds of arrows soaring toward the enemy's front lines. While the arrows are flying through the air, the orcish archers launch a set of their own. Many of the arrows collide with each other in the air and fall to the ground below, but some do make it across to both sides. The first wave hits the orcs hard, killing many of their front-line fighters. Before the arrows reach Genisus, Pelisus pulls his hood off and throws his hands out toward the sky. A large shockwave shoots out from his hands and forms a protective bubble large enough to block the arrows.

The arrows hit the bubble, and Pelisus falls to his knee. Once he has blocked all of the arrows, he erases the bubble from the sky and plants both of his hands on the ground. After seeing Pelisus collapse, Von runs over and grabs him. Pelisus rolls over into Von's arms and is heavily panting; sweat is vigorously rolling down the sides of his face.

"What happened?" Von asks.

Pelisus shakes his head from side to side and quickly snaps back into reality. He stands up and rushes up to the top of the wall to see the enemy army. Pelisus stands up and rushes toward the top of the wall. Everyone watches him, envying his magic and shocked that he is that powerful. As Pelisus reaches the top of the wall, the enemies release another hail of arrows toward the city. Pelisus throws his arms toward the hail of arrows and causes them to immediately stop in the air. Pelisus pants heavily as he turns the arrows around in mid air and thrusts his arms down.

As he thrusts his arms down, the arrows are released from his grip. They fly straight down and into the very archers who fired them. After exerting so much energy, Pelisus falls to his knees again, panting and trying to catch his breath. Just as Von starts to run over to Pelisus again, he hears screams from back at the harbor. Upon hearing the screams, he stops in his tracks and looks down the road. In the distance, he can see one of the guards running toward the front gates of the city.

"There are goblin divers in the back!" the guard screams as he runs toward the front gates of the city.

While the guard runs, Von notices a large spear flying through the air toward him. He goes to yell to him, but it is too late. The spear makes contact with the man's back and immediately takes him down to the ground. Von looks over to Pelisus. who is just starting to stand up again. Pelisus signals for Von to go and that he will be okay. Von nods to Pelisus before pulling out both of his swords and running full speed down toward the harbor.

Right as Von passes the guard's lifeless body, he is able to see all of the attackers coming in from the water. There are a few dark elf boats making their way to the docks of Genisus, but the more immediate threat is the goblins coming in from the water. The goblin divers have gills on their cheeks, allowing them to breathe underwater. Most of them are carrying long, four-foot spears, but some are holding swords or daggers.

Von grips his swords tightly before rushing down to the shoreline, where there are two goblin divers coming out of the water. When they clear the water from their eyes, they notice Von is running straight toward them. They briefly hesitate before running toward Von, with their spears pointing forward. As the first goblin diver thrusts his spear toward Von, he catches it between his right arm and his chest. He swings the sword in his left hand at the other goblin. The blade catches him right across the face, almost removing his lower jaw from his head.

The goblin collapses to his knees and chokes on his own blood as he reaches up and tries to push his jaw back into place. The other goblin looks over at his friend in fear, knowing now what Von is capable of. Von turns his attention back to the living goblin and tightly squeezes the spear against his side. The frail wood that the spear is made out of buckles under the pressure and snaps in two. The goblin releases his grip on the weapon and raises his hands over top of his head before muttering something.

"Not today," Von says out loud before bringing his sword down over the goblin.

The downward thrust cuts through both of the goblin's arms and stops directly in the goblin's skull. Von pulls the sword out of the goblin's skull as the lifeless bloody body collapses to the ground. With the two goblins out of the way, Von rushes up to the shoreline and looks in both directions. Under the pier, he spots four more goblins. They must be waiting for their friends to plan an organized attack; Von bangs his sword against the ground and yells to get the goblins' attention.

They hear the noise and turn to look over. This time, none of them hesitate; they charge at Von, figuring they have a number advantage. Von twirls both of his swords around in the air and cracks his neck while he waits for the goblins to get close enough to kill. The first one that gets near him has a spear, which Von cuts in half with a quick strike. As the goblin stumbles past Von, the back of his neck is met with Von's sharp blade. The strike severs his spinal cord and kills him almost immediately.

The next goblin is met with the feeling of cold steel right through its chest. Von plunges his sword through the goblin. It drops its weapon and takes its last breath of air in. Von lifts the goblin up off the ground and throws it at the other two, as well as his weapon. The goblin's lifeless body knocks the other two backward and on the ground. Von casually walks over to the goblin's body and pulls his sword out. Right after he pulls his sword out, one of the goblins starts to sit up and reach for its weapon again.

Von lunges over to the goblin and shoves his sword through its hand. It yelps in pain, spitting at Von. Von wipes the spit from his armor, bringing his right foot down and crushing the goblin's head. He pulls his sword out of the goblin's hand and starts to walk toward the other goblin, who is now standing up and holding his spear, ready to fight. Von chuckles at the goblin, throwing his sword as hard as possible at it. The goblin raises its spear and knocks the sword out of the air. The sword spirals around in the air, falling toward the ground.

On its way down, it slices open the goblin's leg, causing it to look to the sky and yelp in pain. Von takes advantage of this moment and lunges forward, cutting the goblin's throat open. Its previous yelp of pain is now nothing more than a muffled gargle as its own blood fills its throat. Von picks up his sword and looks down the shoreline. In the far distance, he can see eight or more goblins carrying a small child into the water. The child's body is motionless, which means the goblins either knocked him unconscious or killed him beforehand. Von screams at the top of his lungs, running toward the goblins that are holding the child.

The goblins stop and turn to look at Von, who is running full speed toward them. They see him in the distance. They drop the kid on the hard, rocky ground and grab their weapons. Instead of racing toward Von, the goblins group up and get into a tight formation, readying themselves for him when he arrives. Von charges into the pack of goblins without a care in the world. A few of their swings strike Von's armor, but nothing that could penetrate through.

Von stops in the middle of the goblins and lets out a triumphant yell, spinning around wildly. His swords are extended straight out at both sides as he turns around wildly in one place. The clanging of his sword hitting the other goblins' weapons is almost completely muffled by the tearing of flesh. As Von spins around, blood sprays everywhere, almost covering his face and staining his armor. Upon spinning around four or five times, Von manages to bring himself to a stop and is finally able to get a look around. He notices that half of the goblins are already dead, leaving only four.

The other four goblins are keeping their distance from Von, not wanting to get caught in the whirlwind of metal he just created. "Scared?" Von says in a muffled voice as the goblins continuously circle around him. The goblins start to spread out, trying to keep one of themselves behind Von at all times. It takes about a minute for them to muster up enough courage to try and attack Von, but he already knows what is coming. A loud screech can be heard from behind him, followed by the sound of panicked footsteps.

Von waits a second before turning his swords around, placing them against his sides and thrusting them backward. He thrusts them behind him. The loud screech dissipates and is followed by a final moan of pain from the goblin. While Von is preoccupied with the goblin behind him, the others charge in. The other goblins take a few steps forward; Von rips his swords out from the goblin behind him and begins to swing them around wildly in front of him. He blocks each and every one of their incoming attacks while putting a deep slice in every one of their arms or legs.

With each of the goblins now badly hurt, Von chuckles to himself at how easy it will be. He spins his swords around in his hands repeatedly as he waits for the goblins to make the next move. It doesn't take long for them to grow bored of his arrogance and charge toward him again. The first goblin is met with a strong downward pound on the back of the head, knocking it out cold. The second goblin swings its sword at Von but misses. His bad accuracy is rewarded with a deep slice across then neck from Von's sword. Right after the sword goes across the goblin's neck, it drops its weapon and grabs for the wound.

Blood is spraying out all over the rocks that make up the shoreline. Most of it is caught by the goblin's hands, which are tightly placed over the wound, but some still finds its way to the ground. The remaining two goblins take a few steps back and hesitate on what to do. Without coming up with any better options, they drop their weapons and run off into Genisus. Von decides to let them go, figuring without weapons they will be fairly easy for anyone to kill.

Von walks back over to the goblin he knocked out earlier and grabs him by the ears. He yanks the goblin's head up to look him straight in the eyes. Just at first glance, Von is able to read the fear in the goblin's eyes. The goblin's eyes show that he is begging to be let free and spared.

"Can you understand what I am saying?" Von asks the goblin.

The goblin reluctantly nods to Von.

"Can you speak a language I understand?" Von asks the goblin.

"Yes, little," the goblin replies.

"How do you know of my presence in Genisus?" Von asks the goblin.

"Me no understand," the goblin replies.

"If you answer my questions, I will let you live. Now, how do you know of my presence in Genisus?" Von asks the goblin again.

The goblin swallows hard and thinks over what he is going to say next long and hard. He takes in a long breath of air before continuing, "Big scary pale skin visit dark elves, tell of you and reward for killing you. Big scary man pay well, bags and bags of gold coins, me hear."

"Big scary man? What did he look like?" Von asks.

"Man have red hair, me hear. I don't see him, only hear stories."

"Scarlet ..." Von mumbles out loud.

"Yes! Yes! Dat his name! Dey call him Scarlet!" the goblin replies.

Von releases his grip of the goblin's ears and points out toward the sea to the north. The goblin falls to the ground and looks up at Von. He nods his head and quickly crawls toward the water. When he is fully submerged, he swims away as quickly as possible. With the goblin now gone, Von leans down to pick up his sword. While lifting his sword, he catches a glimpse of a reflection. He tilts the sword back down and notices two goblins approaching from behind him.

These goblins are different than the others. They are both dressed in full black armor, which is covered in seaweed and still has water dripping off of it from the ocean. Their weapons also look to be more fitting for them. They are both wielding inscribed swords, giving Von the impression they are high-ranking officers of their army. Aside from the armor, these goblins look different than the other ones as well. They are much darker blue in color, and their backs aren't arched. Unlike the other goblins, they stand tall, about the same height as Von, and look like they actually can fight. Von grips his sword tightly and spins around to face the two goblins approaching him.

"Surrender now, pale skin, or face imminent death."

"Heh," Von says while he turns down toward the ground. When he looks back up, he has a large smile across his face.

Von readies both of his weapons and charges toward the two goblins. While Von is running at them, they raise their weapons and ready themselves for Von's attack. Von swings his swords violently at the goblins, but each of his attacks is blocked by them. He jumps backward and takes a good look at both of the goblins. Von admires their ability to fight and is happy that he will actually be challenged. "Your turn," Von says with a smile.

The goblins come at Von, swinging their weapons wildly in the air. Each of their attacks is easily blocked by Von. With how fast and accurate the goblins are, Von is unable to provide a counterattack and is only able to defend himself. The goblins keep coming at Von, swinging wildly and forcing him to back up in order to stay alive. Out of the corner of his eye, he notices that he is being backed into a corner, which will be the death of him. Having to think quickly, Von throws one of his swords into one of the goblins' feet. The goblin stops attacking and yelps in pain.

With the other goblin debilitated, Von comes at the other one even fiercer. Each swing ends in the clanging of their two weapons, a sound that echoes across the shoreline and even into the city. While Von is sparring, the other goblin finally grows the courage to pull the weapon out of his foot. Each inch that travels through his foot sends tremendous spikes of pain through his body. When the goblin finally frees his foot from the grasp of Von's sword, he turns toward Von and throws the sword as hard as he can.

The sword spirals through the air at Von. When it is just inches away Von throws his arm behind him and grabs the blade by the hilt. He uses the sword in his left hand to block the goblin's attacks while using the one in the right to deliver a massive blow. Von raises the sword in his right hand up and brings it down on the goblin's neck. The blade penetrates at least a foot down, tearing the torso almost in two. The goblin falls to its knees right in front of Von. Von pulls the sword out and kicks the lifeless body away from him before turning to the other goblin.

"I'll give you five seconds to run," Von says.

The goblin hesitates briefly, knowing that one on one with his injured foot he doesn't stand a chance. Not wanting to back down, the goblin raises his weapon and charges toward Von. Von shakes his head side to side, finding it pathetic that the goblin actually believes he stands a chance. As the goblin reaches Von, he drops the weapon in his right hand and punches the goblin in the chest. The goblin bends over from the blow and is met by an elbow on the back of the head.

This causes the goblin to collapse to his knees. Von walks around the goblin while spinning his sword in the air, laughing at the attempt to kill him. The goblin fully regains consciousness and waits for the perfect opportunity to strike at Von. Right when Von is in front of him, the goblin lunges forward with his sword held high. Von dodges the attack and brings his weapon down right on the goblin's wrist, cutting off his hand and disarming him.

"You should have just run," Von says, kicking the goblin in the face and causing him to fall backward.

Von walks over to the goblin and puts his foot on his chest. He looks down at the goblin and shakes his head side to side before jamming his weapon into the goblin's chest. The blade penetrates through the thick leather armor and straight into the beast's heart. As the sword enters the heart, the goblin attempts to gasp for air but dies before he can even take his last breath. Von pulls his sword out from the goblin and picks his other one up off the ground.

He lets out a long, drawn-out sigh as he turns toward the harbor and notices multiple dark elf boats approaching the docks. Meanwhile, Pelisus is still assisting the guards in the front of the city by blocking the enemy's hail of arrows. Pelisus has successfully blocked three waves of arrows and is getting ready for the fourth when Luna joins him. As the fourth wave of arrows approach Genisus, Luna and Pelisus both throw their arms into the sky.

With both of them working together to block the hail of arrows, Pelisus doesn't get nearly as exhausted as fast as he normally does. Luna and Pelisus team up to block three more waves of arrows from hitting Genisus. Upon blocking all three waves, they both collapse to their knees. The two of them are panting vigorously as the orcs ready themselves for another attack. This time they are loading up the largest catapult they have. They want to test the strength of Pelisus and Luna. See if they can hold back a giant boulder hell-bent on destroying the city.

It takes the orcs and ogres close to five minutes to load the largest boulder they can find into the catapult. Instead of using one that they brought with them, they pick one of the giant rocks from the Genisus Plains. They load the boulder in the launcher and get ready to fire as Pelisus and Luna both push themselves to their feet and notice what is going on. Pelisus struggles to stand as all of the muscles in his body ache from blocking the other hail of arrows.

Luna seems to be struggling too but not nearly as much as Pelisus, since she just joined him. A long, triumphant roar echoes across the orc army as one of them brings their sword down over the rope on the catapult. The orc severs the rope, and the catapult violently swings forward. A large boulder flies through the sky toward the city. The large boulder soars so high into the air that it completely blocks out the sun, momentarily eclipsing the city.

Pelisus and Luna turn to look at each other before lightly nodding. They both take in a deep breath and swallow hard; turning to the boulder and closing their eyes. The two of them extend their arms toward the boulder and move their hands around in the air as they try to stop it. The boulder seems unaffected at first by the magic, but over the next few seconds Pelisus and Luna start to slow it down. Everyone in the city watches the boulder as it slowly comes to a stop in midair.

They turn toward Pelisus and notice that his face is beet red and large beads of sweat are rolling across his forehead. He opens his eyes and starts to breathe violently before baring his teeth. Pelisus keeps his hands pointed at the rock for the next few minutes before throwing them toward the orc army. After performing such an act, both of them collapse to their knees. The rock stands stationary in the air for a few more seconds before shooting back toward the orcs.

All of the orcs run in fear as the giant boulder comes straight toward their army. The boulder flies back to the catapult it was fired from and destroys it like it was made of paper. It bounces a few times after hitting the catapult, running over a few orcs and gnolls, but nothing too severe. Pelisus brings a hand up to his face to wipe the sweat away. While he is wiping the sweat away, he looks at his hand and notices that it is blue again. So much of his energy was used to block the catapult launch that his illusion faded.

It takes the guards a few seconds to notice that Pelisus lied to them and isn't human or elf. When they do, they raise their weapons and turn to Pelisus. Luna stands up and casts a giant blue bubble around Pelisus, making him invulnerable to their attacks for a short period of time.

"You traitor!" one of the guards yells to Pelisus

"He isn't a traitor! He just blocked enough arrows to kill everyone here!" Luna shouts out in Pelisus's defense.

"He was doing that to earn our trust! Now he is going to kill us all!" another guard shouts.

"No! Pelisus is my friend! I won't let you hurt him!" Luna shouts out.

"Ahh, so you're a traitor too? You both shall be killed then!" a guard shouts to her.

"Stop! Everyone stop!" Nunnar, the captain of the royal guard, yells.

"This man has saved all of our lives five times over today, and you want to execute him? What has gotten into you all? This man may be a dark elf and he may have fooled us to gain access to this city, but his heart is good and we, the race of man, do not discriminate based on skin color. What matters is what is in your chest and your head," Nunnar tells all of the guards gathered around the area.

Nunnar walks over to Pelisus, who is standing on top of the walls overlooking the army surrounding Genisus. He stops next to Pelisus and pulls out his sword before gently placing the tip of the blade into the stone below him. Nunnar smiles to Pelisus, getting down onto one knee and placing his forehead against the hilt of the weapon.

"Genisus is proud of what you have done today. We bow to you for your sacrifice and courage in defending our city."

Pelisus manages to pick himself up off the ground and look around the city. Each and every one of the guards is kneeling down to him with their weapons positioned exactly like Nunnar's. A large smile comes across Pelisus's face as he looks around at all of the guards. A tear even rolls down his cheek, but no one would be able to tell the difference between the tear and the sweat.

"Thank you," Pelisus says.

Back at the docks, the first dark elf boat has just arrived. As Von runs toward the boat from the shoreline, he bumps into Lenya right as he reaches the docks. They both smile and nod to each other before continuing north toward the boat that just docked. The dark elf boat is enormous, much bigger than the fishing vessels from the other day. Above the dark elf boat, flailing in the wind is the symbol of their people. It is a large purple flag with a strange black symbol right in the middle of it. As Von and Lenya get closer to the boat, they can hear the large piece of fabric flicking and snapping in the wind.

The two of them continue up the docks until they reach the first wave of intruders, which they quickly engage and dispose of. They make a good team against the first wave of dark elves. Von debilitates them while Lenya finishes them off with quick strikes to the vital places of their body. Once the first set of dark elves is dead, they continue up the docks and toward the dark elf boat. While they are about to board the boat, five more dark elves jump off the side and down to the dock.

Von chuckles before charging into the dark elves. He doesn't even try to kill any of them; instead, he knocks them all over and disarms them so Lenya can finish them off. The first two get a taste of the cold wood beneath them simply by being victims of Von's fists. The other three are quickly met by the plate mail on Von's shoulder or a swift kick to the kneecaps. Whatever it took, once they were on the ground, Lenya quickly finished the job.

With the dark elves out of the way, Lenya races up the ladder with Von and onto the boat. Dark elves are racing around everywhere.

Each of the dark elves on the boat is carrying at least three boxes of supplies. Just as Von and Lenya stop to watch the dark elves, one of the commanders from on top of the watch tower screams out, "Intruders!" His voice echoes across the boat, causing all of the dark elves to stop what they are doing and pull out their weapons, ready to fight.

"You take left, I'll take right?" Von asks Lenya jokingly.

"Sure!" Lenya replies with a smirk.

Von charges to the right side of the boat and starts to flail his swords violently in the air. Within the first ten seconds of swinging, he has already severely wounded half a dozen deck hands, all of which were too inexperienced to defend themselves against Von's attacks. Lenya is making the very same discoveries as Von. With how quick and agile she is, the inexperienced deck hands are no match for her. Lenya is able to plunge her daggers into one of the deckhands multiple times before they are even able to blink.

Von finishes off the deck hands surrounding him, and four experienced elves run up and take arms. A smile forms across Von's face as he looks around at all of the dark elves surrounding him.

"You sure you're ready for this?" Von asks them.

None of the dark elves' facial expressions change after Von speaks. He shrugs and mumbles, "Guess they didn't hear me …" The dark elves hesitate no more and charge in to attack Von. Von raises his swords to block their strikes and is taken off guard by the initial intensity of their attacks. The initial attacks cause Von to stumble backward and catch his balance. With the first few attacks out of the way, the dark elves surround Von and continually walk in a circle around him.

The elves encircle Von; he closes his eyes and waits to hear irregular footsteps. After a few seconds, a set of footsteps stop behind him and close in. Von waits another second for the dark elf to get close and to take the swing at his head. He hears the blade cutting through the crisp air behind him; he drops to his knees to dodge the dark elf's attack and plunges his sword into the dark elf's chest. When he opens his eyes, he looks at the dark elf above him. The elf is frozen like a stone in place, his sword still extended out with Von's deep within his chest.

Blood starts to seep out of his wound and all over Von's sword. Von pulls his sword out and wipes off the blood on the dark elf's clothing before the body collapses to the ground. When he is finished cleaning his sword, he turns around and looks to the three remaining elves.

"Who is next?" Von asks with a slight chuckle.

All three of the dark elves raise their weapons and charge toward Von. They relentlessly swing at Von, giving him no spare time in between blocking their attacks to deliver an attack of his own. As he is fighting, one of the dark elves gets a lucky hit with his fist on the side of Von's head, right over top of his ear. Von stumbles sideways as the fist makes contact with the side of his head. He shakes his head and quickly regains himself. Von raises his weapon to start fighting, and again one of the dark elves strikes his sword so vigorously that it causes Von to fall onto his back. The three dark elves encircle Von and stare down at him.

"Not so strong now, are you, pale skin?" one of the dark elves says as he approaches Von.

"I don't know; why don't you come closer and find out?" Von says.

The dark elves take a few steps closer to Von as he slyly gets ready to swing his weapons at their ankles. Just as he is about to swing at them, one of the dark elves immediately stops in his tracks and collapses on top of Von. His body lands on top of Von; he notices a dagger sticking out of the back of the dark elf's neck. Upon seeing the dagger, Von quickly turns to the left and notices Lenya standing close nearby. Right as Von turns and looks over to Lenya, a small smirk forms across her face.

Without wasting any more time, Von uses the advantage he has against the dark elves. He brings both of his swords together in front of him, through the two dark elves. The blades cut the elves' feet off right above the ankles. The elves collapse backward onto the cold wood of the ship and scream in agony. Von pushes the body off of himself and stands up, using his two swords to silence the screams.

"I had that, you know?" Von says to Lenya jokingly.

"Sure you did," Lenya replies.

"Heh …" Von replies. "Let's go down below deck and find the captain of this boat. Also we can kill any more dark elves we run into on the way to the captain," Von adds.

Lenya nods to Von as following him down into the cargo hold of the ship. They both quickly make their way down a set of rickety wooden stairs and into a very large room with dozens of crates and boxes. Each of the crates has a small white cloth pulled over it, masking the identity of what is inside. Von and Lenya stand at the bottom of the stairs and examine the room, trying to figure out where to go. As they are looking around a large arrow flies across the room and lands in a wooden pillar next to Lenya.

"Down!" Von yells as he grabs a hold of Lenya and takes her behind one of the large wooden crates in the room.

"Do you see him?" Von asks Lenya.

"No … but based on how the arrow is in the wood, I'd say he is in the far end of the room, dead center," Lenya replies.

"That's where he was, chances are he has moved now," Von says. "You go up the right side and I'll go up the left?" Von asks Lenya.

"Deal," Lenya says to Von with a slight smile.

They both split up and slowly make their way through the maze of crates and boxes that litter the floor. Both of them are being extra careful to keep their heads down and out of the archer's line of sight. As Von comes around the side of one crate, he notices a pile of arrows on the ground. Each arrow has a rough, jagged tip and a set of blue feathers on the back end. While he is examining the arrows, he hears Lenya accidentally knocking something over across the room.

Lenya pops her head up after making the noise for a second before having to duck to dodge an arrow from the archer. Knowing that he just fired and will need to restock, Von ducks behind a nearby crate and gets ready for the archer to arrive at his stash. About thirty seconds go by before Von can hear someone shuffling around the pile of arrows nearby. Von leaps out and tackles the dark elf to the ground.

Von quickly places his weapon up to the elf's throat and smiles, slicing it wide open. While the dark elf bleeds out all over the floor, Von stands up and motions Lenya over. With the archer now out of the way, they both look around the room and see if there are any more dark elves to worry about. After a quick glance around, they nod to each other, agreeing that the coast is clear. The two of them return to the stairs and go up one flight, reaching the door that leads to the sleeping quarters.

Von reaches down and turns the door's handle to open the door, but it is locked. Von uses his shoulder to try and make the door budge but still doesn't have any luck. With no other option, Von takes a few steps away from the door and uses his foot to repeatedly kick the knob until it breaks off. The door slowly opens up and reveals a long hallway with doors on each side. At the very end of the hallway there is a staircase leading up, which leads into the captain's room.

Von and Lenya both enter the hallway and quickly make their way toward the stairs leading to the captain's room. The first person up the stairs is Von; he slowly makes his way up the stairs while trying to make as little noise as possible. Lenya follows closely behind Von, constantly checking the hallway to make sure no one is behind them. As Von reaches the top of the stairs, there is another hallway. This hallway is much shorter than the last and only has a single door at the end of it, leading into the captain's room.

At the start of the hallway, Lenya turns to Von and says, "Follow in my exact footsteps and we won't make a sound."

Von nods to Lenya and follows her into the hallway. Throughout the hallway, her movement is sporadic, but she is holding true to her word and not making any noise. Von follows her closely in the hall, being careful not to step anywhere Lenya doesn't. It only takes thirty seconds for Lenya to quietly make her way through the hallway and over to the door on the other side. Von nods to Lenya before opening the door and bursting into the room on the other side.

Waiting for them inside the room is the captain of the ship, dressed in full black clothing and holding a rapier. The captain also has two henchmen at his side, both of them wearing plate armor and holding greatswords. The greatswords they are holding have unique engravings all the way up the blade and even on the hilt. Von is unable to understand what they mean, but they must hold some meaning to the dark elf people.

Lenya and Von spread out as they wait to see if the dark elves want to take the first swing at them or not. A few seconds pass; the captain of the ship lowers his weapon and starts to speak.

"Let's make a deal. You two walk out of here and forget you ever came in here and my friends here won't kill you."

Von turns to Lenya and asks sarcastically, "What do you think? Do you want to die here or walk out the door and go back home?"

"Today seems a like pretty good day to die, but I'm not too sure," Lenya replies jokingly.

Von turns to the captain and says, "How about the three of you use your swords to slit your own throats and then Lenya and I will leave you."

"Ha ha ha, we have a jokester on board," the captain says.

"Dispose of them without making a mess, please," the captain says to his henchmen.

The two henchmen approach Von and Lenya slowly. The fear in their eyes is noticeable as they walk toward their impending death. Von and Lenya both ready their weapons and wait for the dark elves to make the first move. Once the dark elves are within five feet of Lenya and Von, they start swinging their swords violently throughout the air. Von and Lenya dodge each of their strikes instead of blocking any of them. The weight and power of the greatsword is too much to block an attack from.

After around twenty dodged strikes, the dark elves start to become tired from swinging the massive weight of the sword around and pulling it out of the wood it buries itself in. The very next attack at Von is aimed for his head, which Von easily dodges. The sword swings through the air and buries itself in a shelf to the right of Von. Von uses this to his advantage and elbows the dark elf in the nose. The dark elf releases his weapon and stumbles backward as he covers his nose. Fresh blood flows down the elf's shirt and all through his hands.

Von looks at the dark elf and smiles. "Your first mistake was releasing your weapon," he says to the elf, crossing his swords to form and X and pressing them against the dark elf's neck. Von presses down hard and shakes his head from side to side before pulling both of his swords apart and slicing open the elf's neck. The elf collapses to his knees and grabs his neck as death sets in. The dark elf fighting Lenya pauses briefly as he watches his friend die. Lenya takes advantage of the few seconds she has and plunges her daggers deep into the man's chest.

Feeling the daggers enter his body, the man's face goes pale. His eyes ice over in pain as he slowly drifts out of consciousness. With both of the dark elves now dead, the only one left is the captain. The captain holds his rapier up, ready to defend himself. His hand is trembling in fear as he looks at Von and Lenya, unable to hold the rapier straight.

"You slitting your own throat is still an option that is on the table," Von says to the captain.

The captain growls at Von and charges into the two of them while swinging his sword violently. When the captain gets close enough, Von jumps out of the way of his attack and delivers a powerful downward slice to the captain's back. The captain stumbles past Von until finally collapsing onto the ground. Lenya and Von both turn to face the captain's lifeless body and shake their heads at his measly attempt.

After looking at the captain's body, Von turns to Lenya and says, "We should probably get back to Genisus. By now they will need our help again."

Lenya nods to Von as she follows him down and out of the ship. As they both step outside of the ship's underbelly and back into the salty air, the first thing they notice is black smoke billowing up into the sky from all around the harbor. As Von looks around the harbor, he notices that all of the dark elf boats have roaring fires, which have almost fully consumed each of the ships. The only thing left in the harbor is a single boat, which bears a Genisus flag.

This single boat is sailing back toward the city of Genisus from the center of the harbor. Celebrating on the deck of the boat are dozens of Genisus troops. Each of them are proud of the fact that they just singlehandedly took out an entire dark elf fleet. As the ship gets closer to port, they slightly turn toward the ship Von and Lenya are on, realizing it is the only dark elf boat not on fire. As they turn toward the boat, Von runs over to the side of the ship and jumps up on the railing.

He waves both of his hands around in the air and cheers to the boat as they get closer. The men ready their bows until they see a friendly face on board the dark elf ship. A few seconds after seeing Von, they lower their weapons and continue to rejoice in their victory over the harbor. Von lets out a long, drawn-out sigh, happy that there was no confusion or unnecessary bloodshed. As the boat passes by Von's ship, it docks further down, far to the west.

Once the boat docks, the Genisus troops jump off and race back into town, knowing that they are needed at the front. As Von watches them race back into town, Lenya approaches him, and a slight smile comes across her face.

"We should probably get back into town," Lenya says to Von, worrying that they need their help at the front gates.

Von nods to Lenya. "Yeah, you're right. They need our help," Von says before jumping down from the railing.

Von follows Lenya off the boat and onto the long wooden dock, where they see two gigantic ogre berserkers finishing off a group of Genisus' guards. The ogre berserkers stand almost eight feet tall and are wearing heavy metal armor. Both berserkers are viciously swinging their large, two-handed axes around in the air, which slice through the last guard's flesh like it was butter. After the two berserkers finish with the guard, they turn to look down the other end of the dock. A brief pause comes over them as they spot Von and Lenya standing there, but it is quickly interrupted by a bloodthirsty roar and the sound of their pounding feet as they charge toward Von and Lenya.

Von unsheathes his weapons and smiles before he and Lenya charge toward the ogres. The four of them meet in the center of the dock as their weapons clash together and echo across the harbor. Von and Lenya have the upper hand with agility and speed, but the ogres have the upper hand when it comes to raw strength. One blow from the giant two-handed axe that the ogres are holding would most certainly mean instant death.

While keeping this in mind, Von and Lenya dance around the ogres, trying hard to tire them out while avoiding all their attacks. Von tries to swing at the ogres but is unable to get close enough to even reach them. The ogres are too tall and have too much range, making it risky for Von to get close enough to attack. Even with knowing the risk, Von still tries to go for their knees, trying to eliminate their mobility. Each and every attack is unsuccessful.

The ogres stand back to back on the docks, making sure to not let Lenya or Von get to their vulnerable backs. As one of the ogres swings his axe at Von, he brings it down so hard onto the docks that the wood beneath it splinters and cracks. As Von notices this, an idea immediately pops into his head. Von stops circling the ogres with Lenya and now continuously taunts them, wanting them both to swing at him. The ogre is confused at first, not understanding any of Von's hand motions.

Von notices this and coughs a bit before spitting in the ogre's eye. The ogre stumbles backward and growls violently before bringing his axe down right next to Von on the docks. As the axe impacts the wood, it splinters and cracks, exposing the water below. A slight smile comes across Von's face, which he hides from the ogre.

"Come on, you big, stupid piece of shit, let's see what you got!" Von yells at the ogre.

The ogre's face is plain, obviously not understanding Von's language. Lenya starts to catch on to Von's plan, knowing that his intention is to break the wood beneath them and send the ogres into a watery grave. Lenya smirks as an idea pops into her head. She tosses her dagger up into the air and catches it by the blade. She winks and blows a kiss to the giant ogre in front of her before releasing the grip of the dagger.

It flies through the air and the blade lands directly between the ogre's legs, destroying any dignity the ogre had. The ogre collapses to his knees and screams in agony as he reaches down to grab the now bloodied dagger. Not knowing what is going on, the other ogre slightly turns his head, only to see his friend down on his knees in pain. Von takes advantage of this brief moment and attacks. He rushes toward the ogre and plunges both of his weapons deep into his chest. Von lifts the ogre up and pushes him over top the other ogre that is wounded.

The weight of his friend causes him to collapse against the ground and lose grip of his weapon. Lenya grabs her bloody dagger and uses it to quickly end the ogre's life. With the two ogres now dead, Von looks over to Lenya and smiles.

"You ever stab me there and we're going to have a problem," Von says to Lenya.

"Talk about a cheap shot, huh?" Lenya says to Von with a smile.

Von smiles and nods to Lenya. "We should probably get back to the front of the city. Pelisus may need our help."

Lenya nods to Von as she follows him up the dock and back into the city. From the last time they were here, the city has changed dramatically. Now there is a large portion of the houses that are destroyed. There are now shattered windows, broken doors, and large streaks of blood throughout the streets of Genisus. There are bodies lying outside of homes, most likely their owners trying to make one last stand to defend their home from the invaders.

Some of the invaders have started large fires throughout the city, causing large black smoke clouds to billow up into the sky. As Von and Lenya are racing through the city, they can hear the front gates cracking under massive pressure. The enemies on the outside have managed to get their rams close enough to do serious damage to the gate. Von and Lenya can hear the wood of the front gates splintering and finally busting apart as the enemy army charges inside.

While on their way to the front gates, Von and Lenya encounter a pair of dark elf rogues trying to separate a mother and her child. Cries of anguish can be heard from the mother while the child is being drug away into an alleyway. "What do you think you're doing?" Von exclaims when he gets close enough to both the dark elves.

Upon hearing Von's voice, both dark elves stop what they are doing and turn to Von and Lenya. The two dark elves raise their weapons and charge toward Von and Lenya. A small smirk comes over Von's face before looking to Lenya and saying, "Get them to safety, I got these two." Without further hesitation, Von charges at both the dark elves. Each swing of his weapon is met with a quick and agile block from one of the dark elves. As Von is fighting, Lenya runs over to the woman and child and escorts them to safety.

"All right, play time is over," Von says out loud before twirling both of his swords.

Von pulls both of his weapons back and pushes himself forward toward the dark elves. The sound of tearing flesh can be heard as Von easily tears through both of the dark elves. With the two dark elves now out of the way and the mother and child escorted to safety, Von continues toward the front gates. As Von continues up the road, he encounters a goblin shaman as well as an orc berserker bashing in the door to a house. Screams can be heard from inside as the orc berserker makes his way through the door.

"Hey!" Von calls out. "Over here you giant sack of crap!" Von yells out

The orc turns toward Von and lets out a deathly roar, spewing saliva all over the ground. Before Von is able to move, the goblin shaman swings his staff around and causes roots to tear out of the ground and entangle Von's feet. The orc berserker runs toward Von and starts swinging his large, two-handed axe around in the air. The roots continue to grow up Von's legs as he defends himself from the incoming attacks of the orc.

As the roots start to reach Von's chest, he panics and starts to cut away at them. As he takes his attention off the orc, he gets in a lucky attack with the dull side of his axe. The force of the axe causes Von to stumble backward and the roots coming up from the ground to break. Before Von is able to regain himself, the shaman casts another spell and causes a root to break out of the ground and grab a hold of Von's weapon.

The weapon is immediately entangled and stripped from Von's hand. Having only one weapon now, Von continues to defend himself from the orc's relentless attacks. Having to block each of the orc's vicious swings with only a single sword starts to tire Von out. Eventually the orc gets in a lucky attack and causes Von to fall onto his back. The shaman immediately takes advantage of this and conjures roots all around Von's body, almost like nailing him to the ground.

Von raises his weapon and ricochets one of the orcs attack, causing his axe to slice through many roots on the right side of his body. Once all the roots are severed Von grabs his other sword from the ground and rolls out of the way of the orc's gigantic axe. The sword off the ground is quickly thrown at the shaman, causing him to collapse to the ground in a bloody pile.

Von uses his upper body strength and jumps back onto his feet before grabbing his sword from the goblin's corpse. The orc berserker charges toward Von and swings his axe wildly through the air. Before Von is able to block it, the berserker gets a lucky hit on Von's right arm, almost smashing through Von's armor in a single blow. Von falls backward and is met with a strong fist to the face. Von tries to keep conscious as he stumbles into a corner.

The orc gets in a lucky kick, knocking Von deeper into his corner and down on the ground. As Von tries to regain some sort of energy, he can hear the sound of more enemies' feet clanging against the ground, surrounding him. As he stands up and turns around, he notices fifteen or more goblins and orcs standing around him.

Upon seeing all of the enemies around him, he starts to breathe deeply and clench his weapons tight. A slight growl can be heard coming from Von as his eyes start to glow red. A light reddish hue comes over Von's body as his growl gets louder and louder.

"What, what is happening?" Von mumbles to himself. "The power ... is unreal. Is this what the old man meant?"

With the new feeling of power flowing through Von's veins, he charges head first into the enemies. With the new surge of power, Von smashes through enemy forces, killing almost half of them with his initial attacks. Once in the center of all the enemies, Von uses one foot to keep balance while lifting the other one off the ground and spinning around with his swords held out.

Blood flies everywhere as cries of anguish ring out from those caught in Von's whirlwind. In only a matter of seconds, every orc and goblin surrounding Von is on the ground and bleeding out. With everything around Von dead, the red hue slowly fades from him as his grip on the weapons loosen.

"What was that?" Von asks himself. "Was that ... was that my *bloodlust*?"

Von looks up the road and notices enemies are still pouring in through the broken front gates. Knowing they need his help, he runs up the road toward the front gates. He arrives just in time to meet an ogre crawling through the hole in the gate that the ram has made.

Before the ogre is even able to get to his feet again, Von greets him with a blade through the back of his neck.

With the hole now clogged with a fat ogre, the orcs on the other side pull the ram backward and strike again, fully knocking down the door. Von stands in front of the door and fights off as many of the goblins, orcs, and ogres as he can before starting to tire out. Just as he starts to become overwhelmed, the whole sky turns white. Everything seems to slow down and stop around Von as a large flash can be seen in the sky, followed by a very loud explosion.

A large, sandy shockwave is sent toward Genisus, almost one hundred feet in height. The whole orcish, goblin, and ogre army is engulfed in the shockwave as it heads straight for Genisus. Right before it enters the city, though, it stops and dissipates. Now there is a large cloud of dust that covers the Genisus Plains to the south. Many different theories of what is happening can be heard muttered by the soldiers of Genisus. The most common one is that the gods came to help them.

As the dust starts to clear, Von notices that the entire army outside Genisus has been slain. Bodies cover the Genisus Plains, as does broken rubble from their catapults and rams. And none other than Scarlet is walking toward the city. As Von realizes it is Scarlet, he screams for all the archers to open fire on him. They listen and pull back their bows and release a barrage of arrows into the sky. Scarlet chuckles and waves his hand in the air, blocking all the arrows with a magical bubble. The bubble glows red as the arrows make contact with it but otherwise is invisible.

Knowing what Scarlet wants, Von exits the city and walks toward Scarlet. A slight smile comes across Scarlet's face as he sees Von exiting Genisus.

"So, little brother, I see you have learned how to use bloodlust," Scarlet says to Von.

"How do you know about that!" Von exclaims.

"I know about everything, little brother," Scarlet says.

"Stop calling me that! I'm not related to you, you monster!" Von yells to Scarlet.

"Oh, stop lying to yourself, Von, the power of bloodlust runs in both of our veins. Now you know you have this ability. Next question is, can you control it?" Scarlet asks. "Use your bloodlust and fight me!"

Von grips both of his weapons hard and clenches his teeth. He struggles to regain the same power from earlier, but he is unable to.

"Hah! You can't even control it yet!" Scarlet yells out to Von. "Guess I will just have to force it out of you!" Scarlet says.

Scarlet raises his hand and sends out a much smaller shockwave, directed directly at Von. Von is unable to dodge the shockwave and is sent spiraling up into the air. As he makes contact with the ground, both of his weapons are sent flying in different directions. As Von struggles to get up, Scarlet bombards him with another giant shockwave, sending him almost twenty feet across the ground. After Von stops sliding across the ground, Scarlet teleports to him and kicks him into the wall of the city.

Von pushes himself back onto his feet and turns toward Scarlet. Scarlet teleports to Von again and grabs him by the neck before lifting him off the ground.

"Use it! Use the power inside of you, little brother!" Scarlet says out loud.

"Stop it!" a familiar voice exclaims.

Von slightly turns his head and sees Lenya running toward him and Scarlet. "Lenya … No …" Von mutters.

"Oh, you know this girl?" Scarlet says to Von. "Very well then," Scarlet mutters.

Scarlet tosses Von to the side and teleports to Lenya before grabbing her by the neck. Von can hear Lenya gagging as he reaches for his sword.

"Such a pitiful human being," Scarlet says to Lenya. "Did you honestly think you could stop me?"

Von grips his sword tightly and stands up to face Scarlet. His teeth clench together as a red hue comes back over his body. His eyes turn red as he screams at the top of his lungs, "SCAAARLET" before charging toward his brother.

"Finally, you have found the power in you," Scarlet says while releasing the grip around Lenya's neck.

Scarlet jumps up into the sky, almost fifteen feet into the air. While in the air, he extends his arm and sends another shockwave at Von, knocking him back to where he was. Scarlet returns to the ground and begins to walk toward Von, sending shockwave after shockwave at him, continuously knocking him back.

"You're a pathetic excuse for a human being," Scarlet mutters to Von. "Get up and fight!" Scarlet yells at Von before blasting him again.

Lenya begins to run toward Scarlet with both of her daggers drawn. Scarlet lets her get close before turning around and blasting her away with one of his shockwaves. Von watches as Lenya gets blasted away and is immediately filled with anger. He manages to push himself onto his feet and charge at Scarlet. Scarlet laughs at Von's futile attempt and once again blasts him onto the ground with a shockwave.

"You're weak, little brother," Scarlet says to Von. "Perhaps I should come back at another time, when you're more able to fight me."

Just like his entrance Scarlet disappears into thin air, leaving everyone wondering what happened. Von struggles to get up and looks to the sky, which is now returning to its normal color. Unable to keep his eyes open for more than a few seconds, Von leans his head back and passes out.

# Chapter 6
# Lost at Sea

"Guys! He is waking up!" Lenya says out loud.

Von opens his eyes and can only see Lenya's face looking down at him.

"Are you okay? How do you feel?" Von is being bombarded with questions from everyone.

"Well, my head hurts and so does my stomach," Von says before sitting up.

A mirror across from Von's bed allows him to see the bandages wrapped around his head and his chest. In the center of each bandage is a small spot of dried-up blood.

"How long was I out for?" Von asks.

"At least a day!" Luna replies.

"A whole day? We need to get moving then!" Von exclaims.

"No, we're staying here. You need to rest," Pelisus says to Von.

Von pulls the bandage off from his head and feels the tender spot it was covering. "Ouch!" he says after touching the wound. Afterward, Von reaches into his pocket and pulls out the map that Drylor gave to him. He slides the ring down the map and into his hand before opening it up for everyone to see.

"Look, I met someone important on the docks a few nights ago. He gave me this map and told me we need to sail out to this, X" Von tells his group.

"What is at the X?" Pelisus asks.

"The man told me an underwater cave that will contain an artifact I am supposed to bring back to him and the truth about my past," Von says.

"How long do you have to bring back that artifact?" Luna asks.

"He told me to meet him on the docks tomorrow night," Von replies.

"I'll go speak with the dock master about getting us a boat," Pelisus says, encouraging Von.

Pelisus exits the inn and continues toward the docks while everyone else stays back at the inn with Von.

"So what happened after I passed out?" Von asks Lenya.

"We brought you back to the inn and covered your wounds," Lenya replies.

"Yeah! You were hurt pretty bad!" Luna exclaims.

"And Scarlet?" Von asks.

"You don't remember?" Lenya asks Von. "He disappeared right before you passed out."

"Great, more amnesia ..." Von mutters.

Von tosses his legs over the side of the bed and tries to stand up. Unable to stand at first, he reaches to Lenya for aid. She helps him stand up on his two feet and leads him over to his armor.

"Thanks, but I should be fine now," Von says before putting his armor back on.

Just as Von finishes putting his armor back, on Pelisus re-enters the inn and nods to Von with a smile, letting him know they got a boat. Von grabs both of his weapons and sheaths them before leaving the inn. Lenya helps Von along as they make their way to the boat. The boat Pelisus managed to get for them is a very large fishing vessel.

As they walk out onto the docks, there are twenty or so crew members waiting for them. They salute Von and his friends and cheer aloud, calling them the saviors of Genisus. As they walk onto the boat, Lenya helps Von down stairs and lays him down on the first bed she can find.

"You need rest, Von. When we get to the cave, we will wake you," Lenya says to Von

"All right. Here, you will need this," Von says while handing her the map.

"You keep them safe, you hear me, Lenya?" Von says to Lenya, talking about the crew.

"You can count on it," Lenya says to Von with a smile.

Lenya leaves Von in a small bedroom downstairs and closes the door on her way out. As she returns to the top of the ship, Pelisus and Luna are waiting for her.

"How is he?" Luna asks.

"Still a bit shaken up and sore, but I think he will make a full recovery," Lenya replies.

Lenya leaves Luna and Pelisus to go up to the captain's room. Once there, she hands the captain the map to give him a direction in which to sail. After giving the captain the map, she returns to the head of the ship and stares out into the ocean. Soothing sounds of the water gently caressing the bottom of the ship can just barely be heard over the loud mumbling crew. The sea is rather calm, today making sailing enjoyable and easy.

The wind that helps the ship move forward caresses Lenya's face and flutters her hair every time it blows. The smell of sea water fills the air and nostrils of everyone on the crew. Pelisus and Lenya seem to have adjusted to their water legs quickly, whereas Luna seems to be struggling to find hers. For most of the day she can be seen hanging over the railing vomiting up any food she ate the past few days.

As time goes on, Lenya stays below deck in the cargo room sharpening her knives while Pelisus can be found spending his time on the pier looking off into the ocean in front of them. Early in the afternoon, Luna manages to gain her sea legs and makes her way over to Pelisus.

"How much longer are we going to be at sea?" she asks Pelisus.

"Quite awhile. You still feeling seasick?" Pelisus asks.

"A little but not as bad as earlier," Luna replies.

Luna stands next to Pelisus and watches the ocean in front of the ship. Each of the waves slowly rocks the boat side to side.

"It's beautiful," she says out loud.

"Yeah, I've never seen this side of the world. Hell, I never even got out Terrova until Von came," Pelisus says.

"Why did you leave when Von came?" Luna asks curiously.

"I'm not sure, to be honest. I just saw something in the kid that no one else did, and he hasn't let me down since," Pelisus replies.

"I see," Luna replies.

A few more hours pass on the ship before Von wakes up from his nap. He tosses his legs over the side of the bed and cracks his neck before standing up. Von extends his arms and lets out a gigantic yawn before continuing up to the deck of the ship. Once he is topside, he slowly makes his way over to Pelisus.

"How are things looking?" Von asks Pelisus.

"Good for now. We are heading toward a few storm clouds, though, it may shake us up later tonight," Pelisus replies.

"We should be fine. Just keep the boat on course," Von answers.

Von looks out to the west at the setting sun. The colors of red and orange collide with the blue horizon while the remaining heat from the sun is countered by the cool breeze blowing over the ocean. While Von is talking to Pelisus, Lenya comes up from the cargo room and runs over to Von. She tosses her hands around Von and makes it clear how happy she is to see that he is okay.

Meanwhile, the ship continues to sail straight into the storm. Over the next few hours, it starts to rain, only drizzle at first, but it quickly picks up and starts to pour. The once-calm waters start to pick up and violently rock the boat side to side. The only person that seems affected by the roaring waters is Luna, who heads downstairs to try and sleep off her seasickness.

As the night goes on, the storm only becomes worse. Large, twenty-foot waves cascade over the ship, almost washing some of the crew members off. Von is forced to grip the railing as tightly as possible to prevent himself from going overboard. As the boat continues through the storm, loud screeches can be heard in the distance. After hearing the screams, the crew becomes wary about being on the ship.

"Those are the screams of the kraken!" one of the crew members yell out.

"Lies! The kraken is just a myth!" another crew member yells.

"Just a myth you say? Then explain what we are hearing!"

As the ship continues through the storm, the screams get closer and closer as the waves become more and more violent. Just as the storm seems like it will never end, it immediately stops and the waters go calm. The moon once again is visible in the sky, with storm clouds nowhere to be seen. Even the once-feared screams have completely stopped.

"Why ... why did it just stop?" one of the crew members asks.

"I don't know ..." another replies.

As the crew stares off the side of the ship, the water starts to bubble.

"Hey, does anyone see that?" One of the crew members calls out while pointing to the bubbling water.

Before anyone is able to respond ,large tentacles erupt from the bubbling water and grab a hold of the ship. The tentacles entangle the ship and begin to pull it toward the bubbling water. Von immediately pulls out his weapons and starts to cut at the tentacle closest to him. Each slice causes blood to spray all over the deck of the ship. While Von focuses on one tentacle, Lenya and Pelisus each pick another tentacle to attack.

The tentacle Von was attacking snaps in half and retracts itself into the water. Immediately after destroying the first tentacle, he runs over to the second to tear through it. His swords cut through the tentacle like a hot knife through butter, spewing its dark-red blood all over the deck of the boat. After Von finishes with the second tentacle, Lenya and Von work their way down the boat together, destroying the others that latched on.

After the wave of tentacles, a large, eerie face can be seen coming out of the water. The kraken has a birdlike nose and an owl-like face that is bluish in color and covered in barnacles and sea weeds. Its two gigantic eyes stand out as the main weaknesses of the beast.

"The eyes! Aim for the eyes!" Von calls out to everyone on the ship.

Pelisus and Luna unleash spells on the giant beast, hurting it greatly with each hit. They both are using a combination of frost and lightning spells on the kraken, freezing it in place and then electrocuting it. After a few rounds of this, the beast lets out a painfully loud shriek into the midnight sky and submerges back into the waters it came from.

As everyone regains themselves, they take a look around at the boat to see what has been damaged. Von looks around and takes it all in, noticing that almost all of the railings around the boat are shattered but other than that it is only cosmetic damage. Only moments pass before the kraken strikes again. More tentacles grab a hold of the boat and are pulling it toward the bubbling waters, surely to the kraken's mouth. Von and Lenya attack the tentacles on the boat while Luna and Pelisus attack the tentacles coming toward the boat from the other side.

"Melee DPS take the ones on the boat, Ranged DPS take the ones in the air!" Von shouts.

The midnight sky is lit up by the lightning bolts and frost bolts being cast by Luna and Pelisus. Each of them emits a strong light, almost that of a firecracker, until they hit their intended target. They provide just enough light so Von and Lenya can handle any that are already on the deck of the boat. With all four of them working together, they eliminate all of the tentacles that are attacking. Upon the kraken withdrawing his tentacles, he pushes the water and sends an enormous wave toward the boat.

The boat is slammed by the wave and pushed far off course. The wave knocks almost everyone back and even a few of the crew members off into the depths below. Von and Lenya manage to hold onto a broken part of the railing to prevent them from being thrown off. Pelisus and Luna used their magic to block the wave, so much so that they weren't even wet from it. Once the boat steadies again, the screams from the kraken can be heard over everything else.

"The beast, it's coming out of the water!" a surviving crew member shouts.

"Pelisus, cover me!" Von yells out as he runs toward the side of the boat toward the kraken.

Pelisus swirls his staff around in the air and gives Von the power of underwater breathing again. Once in the water, Von swims directly toward the kraken with both swords drawn. While swimming toward the kraken, he slices any tentacles that are left away. Luna and Pelisus start to fire lightning bolts and frost bolts at the beak of the kraken that is above the water. Each hit causes the beast to squeal in pain.

Von reaches the kraken and stabs his swords right in between the beast's eyes. With both his blades in the beast, the kraken ignores the boat and starts to pull Von deep underwater. Von refuses to let go and grips his swords tightly, going along for the beast's ride. A few seconds pass by before the beast hits the ocean floor, the impact almost shaking Von off. Von pulls one sword out and stabs it back into the beast almost two feet away. He then uses his other sword as an ice pick, stabbing it further up and pulling himself along. Each stab into the beast causes it to shriek in pain. Red blood fills the water in front of Von, blinding him from seeing anything else.

The kraken slams into a large rock and breaks large boulders off. One of them hits Von and knocks him off the kraken. Von stumbles across the ocean floor until he can steady himself. Once he does, he pushes off the ocean floor and starts to swim back up to the boat. Von has to swim up for close to a minute before he reaches the surface. From there, he looks around for his boat.

Pelisus and Luna look out to the ocean for Von, not seeing him anywhere.

"Is he alive?" Luna asks Pelisus.

"My spell is still active, so he must be," Pelisus replies.

"Voooooonnnnnn!" Lenya screams out into the ocean.

A few seconds of sorrow pass by until they hear a reply from nearby.

"Guys! I'm here!" Von shouts out.

"Someone get a rope!" Lenya yells to any crew members left alive.

One of the younger crew members grabs a nearby rope and runs it over to Lenya. She grabs it out of his hands and throws one end into the water toward Von while holding onto the other.

"Grab a hold!" she yells out to Von.

Von swims toward the rope and grabs it with his free hand. Once he has a hold of the rope, Lenya pulls him in to safety. Once back on deck, Von lies there and stares up at the sky, catching his breath.

"Are you okay?" Lenya asks.

"What happened?" Luna asks.

"I don't think we will have to worry about the kraken anymore," Von says with a slight chuckle.

The remaining crew members burst into applause at Von's answer, thanking him for saving all their lives. He takes it modestly and waves to everyone before walking off deck back down to the sleeping quarters. When he arrives back in his room, he takes off all of his armor and lies down on the cold, stiff bed. He brings his hand over top of his head and lets out a long, drawn-out sigh. He closes his eyes, but before he can get any rest, Lenya bursts into the room.

"What were you thinking out there!" Lenya yells at Von as she angrily stomps across the floor toward him.

"Huh ..." Von starts to say but is cut off by Lenya.

"You could have gotten yourself killed out there! What were you thinking!" Lenya says to Von.

Von doesn't reply. Instead, he is a bit taken back by Lenya's questions.

"I didn't know you cared so much about me," Von says to Lenya.

"It's not that ... You were reckless today, and we need you, Von. You're our leader," Lenya says to Von.

"I was only doing as a leader should do; I fought off the beast," Von replies.

"I guess ... I guess you're right" Lenya says to Von.

"Now if you don't mind, I could use some rest," Von says to Lenya.

Lenya nods to Von and smiles before standing up and walking out of the room. Von lays his head down and stares at the ceiling. He closes his eyes and takes in a deep breath and lets it out before saying out loud, "Today was a long day ..." After talking to himself, Von nuzzles back into the pillow and tries to get comfortable on the bed. Once he is comfortable, he falls asleep within minutes.

The next morning, Von was awoken by Lenya and the captain knocking on his door.

"Von! We're here!" Lenya calls in to Von.

Von rolls out of bed and starts to put on his armor as Lenya and the captain head back up to the main deck where the others are waiting. Once Von steps out of his room, he can hear arguments from the deck of the ship.

"We're right where the X says, but nothing's here," a crew member says out loud.

"It was a trick, I'm telling you!" another crew member repeats.

"No trick, it's underwater," Von says out loud as he walks up onto the deck.

Everyone turns to Von as he walks up onto the deck and over to the broken railing on the left-hand side of the ship. With Von now awake and up on the deck of the ship, they all wait for his word on what to do.

"Pelisus, give me underwater breathing. I'm going to go find this cave," Von says to Pelisus.

Pelisus nods and swings his staff around in the air before pointing it at Von. Von dives into the water once the spell is done being cast and swims toward the bottom. As he is swimming toward the bottom of the ocean, he passes by a school of fish, which scare as Von passes through them. The water becomes tighter and tighter around Von's body the lower he goes down into the ocean. Almost a minute passes by from when he entered when he finds the ocean floor.

Darkness makes it hard for Von to see, but he spots the large cave the man was talking to him about. Von kicks and paddles his way over to the cave until he finds the entrance toward the bottom. As he swims through the narrow tunnel, he sees a spot up ahead that he can surface at. While swimming through the narrow tunnel, Von tries to keep away from the walls since some of the eels hiding in the holes are almost twice the size of Von.

Once Von makes it to the end of the tunnel, he surfaces and takes a look around the secret cave Drylor told him about. The cave is about twenty feet wide on either side, and it has a very large roof. It's so high Von can't even see how far up it goes. Von pulls himself out of the water and notices a large pedestal in the center of the room. On top of the pedestal is a lantern-looking object. It is most likely the object Drylor asked him to retrieve and bring back to him.

Von walks over to the center of the room where the artifact is and grabs a hold of it. Once he touches the artifact, it shines bright and lights up the whole cave. Water starts to cascade down the northern wall of the cave and cast an image on it. As the water hits the ground, it sparkles into hundreds of different colors, making the area around it look like a rainbow. The image is of a little gnome in the forest around Milem. He is sitting atop one of two horses that are pulling a cart of his along.

Inside of the cart are two wounded soldiers. One of them is Von, and the other is his brother, Scarlet. The gnome is laughing manically and talking to himself the whole way.

"I must get these two back to my lab before they die. I can still save them!" The gnome says in a manic voice.

The vision slowly fades out on the wall before coming back but different this time. This time it shows Von the inside of a building, a laboratory. Scarlet and Von are trapped in two large tubes that have green water filtering through them. Small breathing devices can be seen attached to both of their faces. The gnome from the previous vision is there too. He is typing on the large computer right next to Von and Scarlet.

The gnome walks over to the tube that contains Von and taps on it twice before talking. "You're the lucky one. You actually survived the fire," the gnome says to Von before moving to the next capsule with Scarlet in it. "You, on the other hand, my friend, were killed and should be the most promising of my experiments."

The gnome returns to his computer and starts typing before talking to himself again. "Living test subject was given four vials of my solution," the gnome continues. "The one that died was given thirty times more solution to restart his heart and allow my rejuvenation tubes to take effect."

The gnome walks over to Scarlet and taps on the capsule. "I'm going to call you Project Scarlet; you are the anomaly test subject here that I'm anxious to see awake."

"Also note the green solution they are floating in consists of altered cells of Behemoth, a golem from the underworld and of course a few of my own household chemicals!" the gnome says out loud while snickering.

The gnome returns to the computer and presses a button to record one of his logs. "If all goes as planned, then my test subjects should be awake within a week. Scarlet is alive again, and I do not know if he will retain any of his past self. The other test subject is weak, just barely able to hang in there after infusing him with the cells of Behemoth.

"If all goes to plan, they should be granted massive amounts of strength and the ability to channel their rage into raw power. This is log three for experiment revitalization," the gnome ends with before leaving the room. The vision on the wall ends but quickly comes back with the gnome back in the room.

"This is log fifteen of the revitalization experiment. Scarlet has awakened and is slowly gaining back his memory and strength. He is still extremely weak and can just barely move around in the capsule. There has been no movement from the other man. He will possibly need more time than Scarlet."

The screen of the gnome's records turns to static for a few seconds as you hear a loud crash. The gnome turns around and sees that Scarlet broke out of his tube and is now lying on the floor. The gnome pulls the breathing machine off from his face and tries to hold him up.

"Wait right here, I'll get you something to help with adjusting back to your normal breathing and living."

The gnome quickly runs out of the room and leaves Scarlet alone. Scarlet pulls himself up and wipes the green solution he was just floating in off of his face and anywhere he sees it on himself. When the gnome comes back, Scarlet quickly grabs him by the neck and strangles him until he hears the bones in his neck crack.

Scarlet walks over to the gnome's recording machine and looks right into the camera. The last thing you see is Scarlet's face before everything goes to static.

The water against the wall of the cave glistens before displaying another image. This one is of Von waking up inside the tube. As he wakes up, he starts to freak out and kick the capsule until it breaks and sends him washing out onto the floor in front of him.

Von rips the breathing device off of his face and gasps for air.

"Where … where am I?" Von asks himself.

Von sees the body of the gnome lying by the computer and also the broken capsule that used to be Scarlet's. Von brings his hand up to his head and lays it across his forehead. "Who … I don't even know who I am," Von says out loud in a very depressed voice.

The vision shows Von standing up and leaving the building the gnome brought him to. As he leaves the laboratory, he stumbles out into woods. It is dark outside, making travel through the woods extremely difficult. Von stumbles over logs and through all the shrubbery in the woods. The vision cuts in and out as Von walks through the woods, not showing any part for more than three seconds. When the morning sun is on the horizon, Von spots a hut in the distance. As he arrives at the hut, he collapses on the front patio.

The owner of the hut, an old man, hears the noise and steps outside. He sees Von collapsed on the front deck of his house and decides to drag him inside and help him out. Later that day, Von awakens in the old man's bed.

"Glad to see you're awake!" The old man says to Von.

"Where … where am I?"

"You're in the Misty Woods at my hut. What's your name, lad?" the man asks.

"I don't … I don't know," Von replies to the man.

"Well you can call me Bornek," the man replies.

"What are you doing living out here in the Misty Woods? Isn't this dark elf lands?" Von asks curiously.

"I was once a member of the Genisus Royal Guard, and I wanted to retire far, far away," Bornek replies.

"I see. Thank you for being so kind and helping me," Von replies.

"No problem. You scared me this morning, though, when I heard the loud thump on my patio. I thought the dark elves finally got ballsy and came to my house.

"So you lost your memory lad? The best part is to start with what you do remember," Bornek says to Von.

"I don't remember anything, though," Von says to the man.

"That's okay, lad, I'm sure it will all come back to you in time," Bornek says to Von.

The older man sits pulls up a chair next to the bed and sits down with Von. He tells him stories of his days in the Genisus Royal Guard. He tells stories of combat and battle as well as love and desperation. Von admires the older man and listens closely to each of his stories. Each of the man's stories sounds more and more like what Von thought he remembered from his past.

After telling Von a few stories, the older man shows Von his full suit of Genisus Royal Guard armor. Von admires the armor that Bornek shows to him. Each piece of armor is still gleaming from being recently polished. The full suit of armor is still in perfect condition, regardless of how old it is. Von listens to a few more of the man's stories before lying back down to rest. Bornek continues to speak about his glory days while making some squirrel soup for himself and Von.

Von inhales the soup, since it is the first thing he has eaten in weeks.

"That should help you get some strength back," Bornek says to Von.

Von nods to Bornek and thanks him for the soup. Von decides to only spend another day at Bornek's house before it is time to leave. With Von now fully recovered and ready to go, he tells Bornek thank you for allowing him to stay and for feeding him. The old man nods and hands Von his full set of Royal Guard Armor.

"A present to you. You'll need this armor if you want to make it out of the woods alive," Bornek says to Von.

"I can't accept this," Von says to the man.

"Don't worry, lad, I have no use left for it!" Bornek says to Von.

Von accepts the man's gift and leaves the hut, entering the Misty Woods. Bornek wishes him safe passage and warns him of the dark elves in the area. Von thanks him and exits Bornek's house, heading north through the Misty Woods.

The vision being cast inside the cave ends now that it has fully explained Von's past to him. Von takes the artifact Drylor asked for and stuffs it into his pocket before jumping back into the water and swimming back up to the ship. Once he surfaces, Lenya tosses him a rope to grab onto, and everyone helps pull him back onto the boat.

"Well, I got what Drylor asked for," Von says to everyone while holding up the artifact.

"We should make haste in getting back to Genisus. I don't want to keep him waiting," Von says to the captain.

The captain nods before returning up to his chambers and turning the ship around. Von takes the artifact back out of his pocket to inspect it once more before heading back to Genisus. The artifact glimmers in the light of the day, almost painful for the eye to look at.

"So that's it?" Lenya asks.

"What do you mean?" Von replies.

"You went down there, under the water, for that little thing and that's what this mysterious man asked you to do?" Lenya asks Von in an obviously upset voice.

"No, I learned about my past while I was down there. I know who I am now," Von replies to Lenya.

"Now if you will excuse me, I could use some more rest," Von says before walking off the deck and toward the sleeping quarters.

Von walks through the inner part of the boat back to his sleeping quarters, where he stares at the artifact quietly. He carefully examines each side of it as well as the top and bottom, trying to figure out why Drylor would want to collect any of these. Von continues to quietly examine the artifact for close to an hour before finally lying his head down and getting some rest. Von manages to sleep through the whole day until they dock back in Genisus later that evening.

All the commotion from on top of the ship wakes Von out of his slumber. He stumbles out of his bed and continues back up to the deck of the ship where everyone is waiting. Upon walking out onto the deck, Von takes a look at the evening sky. The sun is just starting to set; luckily they made it back in time to meet Drylor later that night.

Lenya stays back on the ship with Von while Pelisus and Luna leave for the inn to reserve their room for the night. All of the crew members leave the ship to see their family and tell stories of surviving against the kraken. Von walks up to Lenya and puts his hand on her shoulder.

"Sorry for being so rash earlier. I didn't mean to upset you," Von says to Lenya.

"Don't worry about it. I was being nosey," Lenya replies to Von.

Von and Lenya both hop off of the boat and start to walk back toward the inn. As they pass the crew members and their families, they run over and thank Von and Lenya for helping defeat the kraken. Back at the inn, Pelisus and Luna are waiting for them.

"So, Von, you're running out later tonight at about twelve to give the artifact to Drylor?" Pelisus asks.

"Yes, and in return he should give me the location of Scarlet," Von replies.

"How do we know we can trust him?" Pelisus asks.

"We have no other choice. No one else knows the location of Scarlet," Von answers.

"You're right," Pelisus replies.

Von takes an available seat on one of the beds before kicking his legs back and lying down to stare at the ceiling. Before anyone can get rest, a loud knock can be heard at the door to their room. Luna anxiously runs over to the door and opens it up to see who it is. A courier stands at the door dressed in royal clothing.

"Sir Von and his companions, the king would be honored to have you join us at the castle for dinner tonight," the messenger says to everyone in the room.

"Tell the king that we would be honored to join him for dinner," Von says out loud to the courier.

"Then please let me know when you are ready to leave and we can begin toward the castle," the courier says to Von.

Von stands up and brushes off his damaged armor before smiling and saying, "We're ready to go now."

"Very well, then, follow me," the courier says to everyone.

Everyone stands up and exits the room behind the courier. The courier leads them out of the inn and down the main road of the city toward the castle. Around this time, most of the shops are closing their doors and locking up for the night. That is, any of the shops not damaged from the attack a few days ago. After passing the shops, they enter a large residential area where the upscale members of society live.

Next to some of the mailboxes outside the houses are bouquets of flowers, probably put there by the friends and families who lost someone during the attack. They continue following the courier all the way up until they reach the castle. As they're approaching the castle, the gates open up, letting everyone know that they're expected inside the castle.

The courier leads them through the halls of the castle, passing royal guards all along the way. Each of them salutes Von and bow to him as he passes, both for saving the city and for wearing the same armor as the guards. Shockingly, the inside of the castle is still in perfect condition after the battle a few days ago. The large stone pieces that were used to build the floor and walls are all still clean and just recently polished too.

Hanging along the walls every few feet throughout the hall is a piece of carpet bearing the Genisus symbol, two swords with a shield placed over the hilts. They continue down the hall until the very end, where it dumps out into a very large, oval like room that is the dining room. At the head of the table sits the king, welcoming everyone with a wave.

"I'm glad all of you could join me for dinner tonight. I hear many of your stories throughout these halls," the king says to everyone just joining.

"Thank you for having us," Von replies to the king.

Everyone takes a seat around the table and passes each other any nearby foods to help fill the plates. After the initial confusion of everyone passing around dishes is over and everyone is safely able to dig into their food, the king taps on his glass to begin an announcement.

"I would like to again thank all of you for joining me tonight. I would also like to thank you for your valiant defense against the invading army when they came to Genisus. I hear that it is the four of you I must thank for our army being victorious," the king says to the whole table.

Everyone inside the dining room, including the servants, applauds after the king is done speaking. Von looks over to Lenya and can see a slight amount of red come across her face as she blushes from all the attention.

"I do have one question, however," the king says. "Von, what can you tell me about the man you fought just outside our gates the other day? The man with long red hair."

"That man is named Scarlet, and he is my brother," Von says out loud.

Gasps fill the room after Von finishes speaking.

"Your ... brother?" The king asks curiously.

"Yes, but as you can tell, I don't like him at all, and it is my goal to stop the evil he has brought to this world," Von replies to the king.

"That is a relief to hear," the king says out loud. "Is there anything we could do to help you in your journey?"

"Sorry, but it is one I must do alone," Von says to the king.

"Understandable," the king says to Von.

Von and the others continue to eat the food quietly at the dinner table. Each of them is sure to use their best manners and not disturb anyone else while eating. All conversation dies off during the meal; everyone is too busy eating the delicious food brought to them from the royal cooks of the castle. At the end of the dinner, everyone thanks the king for having them and is escorted back to the inn. It is now dark outside, right around ten at night.

Back at the inn, everyone stands in silence and waits until it is time for Von to walk out onto the docks and meet with Drylor. When the time comes, Von stands up and exits the inn alone. He walks out to the most northern dock where he met with Drylor before and waits. Around midnight, a cloaked man comes walking up the docks toward Von. Von takes the artifact out of his pocket and holds it in his hand as Drylor approaches.

"So, I see you have my artifact," Drylor says to Von once he gets close enough.

"That I do. Now I believe you have something for me, correct?" Von says while handing Drylor the artifact.

"That I do. Here is a map that will take you to your brother," Drylor says, handing Von a map. "He knows you are coming," Drylor says to Von.

"Good, then he will know what killed him," Von says to Drylor before starting to walk away.

"Wait! There is something else I must tell you," Drylor says to Von before stopping him by grabbing his shoulder.

"Scarlet has become a plague to this world; a plague that must be stopped. Von, only you have the power to defeat him. Within your bloodlust is the strength you will need to channel in order to defeat your brother."

"I understand," Von says to Drylor.

"Then you may go," Drylor says to Von.

With the exchange out of the way, Von heads toward the front gates of Genisus, bypassing the inn, as he plans to try this task alone. As he reaches the front gates of the city, Lenya comes out from the shadows in a nearby alley way.

"Thinking of leaving us behind, Von?" Lenya asks.

"It is a dangerous mission. I am going to do it alone," Von says to Lenya.

"I'm sorry, but I can't let you do that," Lenya says to Von. "We've come all this way with you; are you so foolish to think we care about the danger ahead?" Lenya says to Von in an angered tone.

"Lenya … I'm not here to put more lives in danger; I'm leaving to save the world from Scarlet's evil. My goal is to protect people like you that I care about and to protect people who can't protect themselves."

Before Lenya can respond, Pelisus walks down the road toward Von and says, "You're not leaving here without me, Von!"

Von turns around and notices Luna running up the road right behind Pelisus.

"You can't get rid of me that easily either!" Luna shouts out.

"Von, return to the inn and stay the night with us. Then in the morning we will leave together as a team," Lenya says to him.

Von looks around at all of his friends surrounding him, begging him not to leave. With no other logical options, Von puts his head down and sighs. "All right, we will leave first thing in the morning." There is a small amount of cheer that breaks out from Luna and Lenya, who are glad that Von came to his senses and waited for them.

Von follows them back to the inn, where he lies down and rests for the night. First thing in the morning, Von looks at the new map Drylor gave him to learn of Scarlet's location.

"All right, everyone, listen up. Scarlet is located at Mt. Fornal to the west. It is at least a three-day journey. We will be traveling across the Genisus Plains until we reach the Ochre Plains, which will take us to the base of Mt. Fornal," Von says to everyone.

With the path now set in stone, everyone grabs anything they brought with them to the inn before heading downstairs to check out. They continue through the city, all the townsfolk making way as they come through. Cheers and applause can be heard among the townsfolk as often as whispers and comments about Pelisus and their defense of the city. At the front gates of the city, the king awaits them to wish them a safe voyage and to give them a gift.

"Von, may I have a moment with you?" the king says to him.

Von and the king step aside from everyone else. The king pulls Von close and whispers into his ear.

"Take this amulet. It will help protect you. It has been handed down through my people for centuries, and as the story goes, the one who saves Genisus is to bear this amulet," the king says to Von while handing him an amulet.

The amulet fits in the palm of Von's hand and is large and circular, set with a sapphire stone in the center of it. The amulet gleams in the light of the day, almost blinding Von as he looks at the gemstone. Von thanks the king for his amulet and proudly puts it on in front of him. The king places his hand on Von's shoulder and wishes him safe passage before stepping back and letting him go.

Von turns around and nods to all of his friends, letting them know he is ready to continue. The plains of Genisus look completely new now that Scarlet annihilated the enemy troops that once filled the plains. Scattered shrapnel from destroyed rams and catapults can be seen all over the plains. Most of the pieces are small, but occasionally the crew passes one that is still mostly intact. The piece of the catapult towers over top of each of them and arches over the path they're following away from Genisus.

The once-tall grass of Genisus Plains is now pushed to the ground. The giant shockwave was strong enough not only to bend the grass to the ground but also force it to stay put. Von leads everyone southwest down the beaten path through the plains. Travel this time is much easier, as there is no tall grass to trek through. The destruction continues on for a while through the plains. As they continue to travel through the plains, the amount of bodies starts to decrease. In the morning sun, the stench of death can be smelled across the plains.

All along the path large portions without any grass can be seen. Usually sitting next to the large portions without the grass is a large boulder, having just barely moved from the large shockwave earlier. Von and the group traveled across the Genisus Plains until about midday, when they reached the large fence separating Ochre Plains from Genisus Plains. The fence is very old and busted in so many places that it barely still serves its purpose.

On the other side of the fence, the tall grass is golden in color. It is almost as if the Genisus Plains and Ochre Plains share different seasons. While the Ochre grass is golden in color, the grass from the Genisus Plains is still green and lively. Von steps over the fence leading into the ochre plains and helps the others across before continuing southwest toward where the map shows Scarlet.

"How far are we going to be going?" Lenya asks out loud.

"We are heading to Mt. Fornal far to the southwest. Scarlet will be waiting in a cave on the mountainside; according to Drylor, he expects our arrival," Von says out loud to the group.

"How much farther is it?" Luna asks impatiently.

"We still need to travel across the Ochre Plains and over to Mt. Fornal. It is probably a two-day journey," Von says out loud.

They continue through the Ochre Plains. Travel is much harder now with the taller grass, but Von manages to keep a steady pace while traveling through the plains. Throughout the Ochre Plains stand large oak trees, many of them towering far more than thirty feet up into the air. These trees are made home by the large ochre birds that the plains were named after. The birds are no threat to normal passersby, but if disturbed, they have been known to attack on more than one occasion.

Von stops under one of the large oak trees around dinner time for a quick break. Everyone takes a seat around the tree and stares off into the golden Ochre Plains that surround them. As the wind blows across the plains, a small amount of pollen can be seen blowing across the top of all the tall grass. Small chirps from baby ochre birds can be heard up in the oak tree they are staying under.

"Anyone else hear that?" Pelisus asks.

"Yeah, it's an ochre bird above us. Don't worry, if we don't provoke it, it won't bother us," Von says to Pelisus.

Moments later, the giant bird flies out from the tree and out into the Ochre Plains around them. The bird's wingspan is gigantic, almost four feet in length. Loud screeches can be heard coming from the ochre bird as it flies across the plains in search of food. Everyone stares and watches the majestic beast as it circles its prey in the distance before finally swooping down to claim it. Once the bird has its prey captured and subdued, it flies back to the tree and lands next to the nest.

After watching the bird feed its young, the small group of adventurers grabs their supplies and once again continues on the long journey toward Mt. Fornal. Von looks up into the setting sun and can just barely see the mountain in the distance. A large red ring can be seen around the mountain's peak, an obvious indication something vile is going down there. Large smoke is seen billowing out of the top of the volcano atop Mt. Fornal, and the cloud cover is just enough to see the mountain in the distance.

As the trek continues, each of them start to become exhausted from pushing all the grass out of their way. Small complaints can be heard from everyone aside from Von, who seems hell bent on reaching his brother.

"When are we going to take a break for the night?" Luna asks in an exhausted voice.

"Soon, when the sun is almost down we can stop and make camp for the night," Von says to Luna, hoping to calm her nerves.

"But I'm tired now!" Luna says in an angered voice.

"Well we can't stop yet. We still have some ground to cover in these plains," Von says to Luna.

Luna mutters something incoherent under her breath as she continues to follow Von toward Mt. Fornal. They continue toward the mountain until later that evening. Once the sun is almost fully behind

Mt. Fornal in the distance, Von finally decides to stop for a rest under a nearby oak tree. He collects a few sticks and fallen branches from around the tree and starts a small campfire for everyone to gather around. Everyone lays down their weapons and gathers around the small fire to enjoy the last few minutes they have before sunset.

"So, Von, how do you plan to stop your brother?" Pelisus asks curiously.

"I'll use my bloodlust to stop him," Von remarks to Pelisus.

"I don't mean to sound negative here, but you can't even control it," Pelisus says to Von.

"I'll figure out how," Von says while shaking his fist in the air.

"Von, you can't surely—" Lenya begins to say.

"Look! This is my fight. I have to win it ..." Von says before turning away from everyone and walking away.

Von walks over to a log on the other side of the tree and sits down. Meanwhile, he tosses any rocks he finds by the log far off into the distance.

"What are we going to do? Von still doesn't know how to control his bloodlust," Luna says to the group.

"If he can't control it, how can we possibly expect him to save the world?" Lenya says out loud.

"Have you seen Scarlet? Von doesn't stand a chance alone," Pelisus says to Lenya and Luna.

"Some of his magic is more powerful than I could ever hope to achieve," Pelisus says out loud.

"I have hope in Von ..." Lenya says out loud.

Von stands up from the log and starts to pace back and forth. Surges of emotions rush over him, ranging from anger to guilt. As Von fights off his inner demons, the conversation continues on the other side of the tree.

"All that it takes is for him to get angry right?" Luna asks.

"Yeah ... but ..." Lenya starts to reply but is unable to.

"Well then all we have to do is piss him off!" Luna shouts out.

"Look! We can't just expect to throw Von at Scarlet, piss him off, and expect him to win! Von isn't a puppet!" Lenya yells to Luna before stomping off to go see Von on the other side of the tree.

Von hears Lenya coming and takes a seat back down onto the log as he waits for her. Lenya walks up and sits down on the other side of the log before putting her face deep into her hands. She breaks her hands away and lets out a long sigh before looking to Von.

"How are you feeling?"

"Anxious."

"That's as expected. After all, you're going after your brother now."

"I just feel like … like I can't do it …" Von says to Lenya.

"Look, Von, maybe this isn't your fight—" Lenya starts to say to Von but is quickly interrupted.

"This *is* my fight! You saw what he did to the entire army outside of Genisus. Imagine if he used that power to harm people instead of just playing around with me and treating me like his toy doll," Von yells to Lenya.

Lenya approaches Von and takes a seat on the log next to him before putting her arm around his shoulder. She turns to him as a small tear runs down her cheek before speaking.

"Von, maybe you're just not ready to fight Scarlet …"

Von slowly starts to speak again, "No. I saw this vision of me and my brother. A gnome genetically altered us. He used us as test subjects. I'm the only one with the power to defeat my brother … It has to be done."

"Genetically altered … how?" Lenya asks.

"I don't know. All I remember is waking up in a capsule with green water all around me and breaking free. I have no idea what tests were done on me or anything."

"Well, Von, if you really think you can take on your brother, then we should continue our journey in the morning, but for now we should get some rest."

"You're right," Von replies. "All we can do tonight is rest. We have a long journey ahead of us tomorrow."

With that being said, Von and Lenya both return to the group and sit around the campfire they have started. For the rest of the night, everyone is silent and calm. Occasionally one of the group members will use a large stick they found to poke the fire and keep the burning hot red coals on top. By the time midnight rolls, around everyone is asleep except for Von.

Thoughts of having to fight his own brother in the days to come worry him so much that it is difficult for him to sleep. Is he ready? Can he figure out a way to control his bloodlust? How many lives are in danger if he doesn't do this? All of these are questions Von is asking himself as he tries to fall asleep. After many hours of pondering to himself, he finally closes his eyes and gets some sleep before the morning.

Everyone is awoken around eight in the morning by the chirping of the ochre birds above. The sun is just rising and casting its glow over the entire plain. The mother ochre bird is out looking for food, while the babies consistently squawked, waiting for her to come back with some their delicious meal. Von is the first to wake up and sit up, rubbing the sleepiness out of his eyes. Everything is still this morning; even the campfire is almost completely out from the night before. As Von shuffles around to stand up, he winds up waking everyone else up at the campfire.

As everyone wakes up from their slumber, they yawn and stretch their arms, getting ready for the long journey ahead of them. Von picks up both of his weapons and sheaths them as he waits for everyone else to do the same. Once everyone is ready, Von leads them through the Ochre Plains, continuing southwest on his journey.

They walk over the rolling hills of the Ochre Plains, just barely able to see over top of each one from the long brown grass that comes up to their waists. As the day goes on, the strength of the wind increases. At first it is a small, simple calming breeze, but eventually it becomes a deterrence to their journey. Each of them is forced to shield their eyes from the wind, which is blowing small particles off the long, tall ochre grass.

Each gust of wind feels like a tidal wave pushing them from side to side as they try to navigate through the field. As time goes on, the gusty winds only get worse. After a few hours on foot, they can finally see the path leading up to the Mt. Fornal. Around the top of the large mountain is a very large smoke ring noticeably different than the surrounding clouds. As they continue their journey through the Ochre Plains, the winds calm down the closer they get to the mountain.

But the closer they get to the mount, the more dread they feel upon themselves. Everyone can sense Scarlet's evil presence inside of Mt. Fornal. It is dusk by the time they reach the path leading up to Mt. Fornal.

"All right, everyone," Von says out loud. "We are going to make camp here for the night, and then tomorrow we will continue up to face Scarlet."

The weary travelers lower their packs to the ground and find a comfortable place to sit for a moment before collecting wood for a fire. The trees in the area are scarce, but Von finds the perfect one to make camp under. After the short breather, everyone gets up and starts to collect any wood, leaves, or other flammable objects they can use to start the fire. While everyone is searching for firewood, Luna finds something even better.

"Hey, everyone! Over here!" Luna calls out.

Everyone stops what they are doing and walks over to Luna, who is crouched down next to a bush with bright red berries.

"What did you call us for?" Von says with a smirking smile and ill-conceived sarcasm.

"It's an ash berry bush!" Luna says to everyone, "They're the only edible berries around here, and I figured it would be a nice snack for us all since we don't have any food and since there are no animals to hunt."

"Are you sure they are safe?" Lenya asks.

"Yeah! Watch!" Luna says before picking a berry off the bush and putting it into her mouth to chew it up.

Everyone watches Luna as she eats the berry and then smiles to them, her teeth slightly red from the berries.

"Well, some food is better than none at all, I guess," Von says.

Von walks over to the bush and starts to pull off berries and eat them. Pelisus and Lenya follow in his footsteps and do the same. Small conversation is made while everyone is munching away at the ash berries Luna discovered. After their dinner session, everyone returns to collecting firewood. While collecting firewood, this time Pelisus finds something of interest. He calls everyone over and shows them two abandoned tents on the other side of a very large rock. The tents are light and moveable, so the group carried them over to the tree they would be spending the night under.

With the tents in place and the campfire now lit, everyone gathered around it for the last time.

"So, are you anxious about tomorrow, Von?" Luna asks.

"Yeah … I won't lie. I just hope I can control my bloodlust and defeat him."

"I have trust in you," says Pelisus

Von nods his head. "Thanks, good friend. Thank all of you, actually, for coming along with me. I don't think I could have done this alone."

"You're welcome," everyone replies almost at once.

As time passes on, everyone watches the crackling fire. The reds, oranges, and even blue flames that are coming out of it seem to keep everyone's attention for the remainder of the night. Pelisus opts to stay on guard for the night while Luna and Lenya share the same tent and Von gets one all to himself.

Von lies by himself, staring up at the top of the tent, which has a small opening allowing a sliver of moonlight into his tent. Nothing worried him more than tomorrow, which could very well be the last day of his life. Von takes in many deep breaths, breathing in through his nostrils and out through his mouth to calm himself down. Moments later, is was asleep

Over in Lenya and Luna's tent, Luna is sound asleep. Lenya keeps tossing and turning, knowing what was to come tomorrow. Close to an hour passed before Lenya decides she isn't going to get much sleep tonight and quietly sneaks out of her tent. Pelisus is outside meditating by the campfire, so Lenya sneaks by him and over to Von's tent.

Von is sound asleep when Lenya walks in to wake him up.

"Huh …. What are you doing in here?" Von barely mumbles in a just-awoken voice.

"I couldn't sleep," Lenya says to Von.

Lenya brushes Von's golden brown hair away from his eyes and looks him straight in the eye. A large smile comes over her face as she leans in to kiss him. Von happily accepts and kisses her back.

They lock lips for a few seconds before breaking and staring at each other in silence.

"Lenya ... I ..." Von started to say.

"Don't say anything Von," Lenya replies.

The two of them both slowly get undressed while exploring the insides of each other's mouths. As each piece of clothing comes off, it is pushed into a small corner of the tent. Once they're both naked, Lenya gets on top of Von and places both her hands on the sides of his face. She leans in to kiss him as she rocks back and forth on top of him. Von moans in pleasure in between the kisses, as does Lenya. Over time, their bodies being pressed together causes them to sweat and slide up and down across each other much more easily.

Von reaches down and puts his hands on Lenya's hips and helps her movements by making his own. Each of them is now sweating as they make love to one another. Lenya reaches down and slightly nibbles on Von's ear, teasing him and causing him to thrust harder and harder into Lenya. They explore each other's bodies, endlessly finding each point to turn each other on. As they continue, they become even more sweaty, and their heartbeats quicken. They can't help but pant for air, stopping all kissing between the two of them. Eventually it happens; Von releases himself of all his worries and stress and gave Lenya the exact same thing.

The two of them feel free: free of anxiety, free of control, and free of responsibility. Their bodies collapse on one another as they both catch their breath. Time passed, with both of them just resting on top of each other, Von still inside of Lenya and Lenya still on top of Von. Von never felt so relaxed and at ease with the world. He also now has the courage within himself to fight his brother Scarlet and defeat him.

A few more minutes pass before Lenya pulls herself up off of Von and puts on her clothes. Von follows her example and puts his tunic and pants back on. Lenya once again sneaks out of the tent and past Pelisus and over to her original sleeping arrangement. Both of them know they want to keep this their dirty little secret.

# Chapter 7
# The final Confrontation

Around seven in the morning, Pelisus goes around and wakes everyone up to prepare for the long journey still ahead of them. The path this time, though, is much different than the others. Now they are walking up long, windy, steep paths with large rocks dotting their way along them. They can tell this is a very infrequently traveled path due to no caravan marks and very little reason to even go up to Mt. Fornal. As they walk, they pass an occasional ash berry bush, where they stop and harvest as much as they can for some nutrition on the journey.

As they go higher and higher up the mountain, their vision decreases. They start to enter the large smoke ring. The trek is hard, especially for Luna, since her legs are much shorter than the others, and getting over some of the larger rocks required help from someone else lifting her up. But they manage. As they round the large northern bend of the mountain, they notice a river of lava flowing down in a valley next to them, something that would surely mean certain death if they fell in. Higher up the mountain, it started to rain down ash on top of the group.

It was nothing that could hurt them but more of a nuisance that they had to deal with. Everyone uses their tunic to or robe to cover their noses and mouths to prevent breathing any of it in. As they continue up the volcano, the ash thickens and makes it hard for everyone to see where they are going. They seem almost lost until dusk set in, when they found an entrance to a cave leading inside of Mt. Fornal.

They all step inside the cave and take off their protective breathing regiments before patting each other down to clear off all of the ash. They look around the cave and notice it is long, narrow, and straight, with torches lit all the way down, meaning someone had to have been here recently and maybe was even expecting company. The brave adventures continue down the tunnel, following the line of torches that light their way. At the end of the tunnel, they find a long, wooden, rickety bridge leading across a dangerously deep gully.

"All right, guys, we should probably go across this bridge one by one because who knows how much weight it can hold," Von says to the group. Everyone nods in agreement.

Von is first to cross the rickety bridge. He takes each step carefully and tries to avoid the wooden boards that look old or rotted. Once Von makes it across, he waves on Lenya to come next. Lenya balances her way across the bridge and slowly makes it across, just like Von. Next up is Luna. She easily makes it across the bridge, barely shaking it because of her size. Last is Pelisus. He walks across the bridge slowly toward the other side, but as he is walking across, one of the wooden ropes he is using for support snaps.

Pelisus drops his staff and holds onto the rope with both hands as he swings over to the side Von and the rest of the group are on.

"Just hold on, Pelisus, we'll pull you up!" Von shouts before grabbing the rope holding Pelisus and pulling on it.

Lenya and Luna lend a hand in pulling Pelisus back up to more sturdy ground. Once everyone is across, they let out a deep sigh of relief.

"Well, I guess there is no turning back," Pelisus says sarcastically,

Von nods. "Let's continue."

In front of them now is another long, windy tunnel with torches. Von and Lenya pull their weapons out, not knowing what to expect further on in the tunnel. As they continue down the tunnel, a low humming can be heard; the deeper they go, the louder the humming. The tunnel leads them spiraling down deep into the center of Mt.

Fornal. As they continue deeper through the tunnels, a faint blue glow can be seen around even turn. It gets brighter and brighter as the brave adventurers continue on.

Eventually they come out into a large room with a small stone bridge going across with a giant platform in the middle. Surrounding the platform is about a fifty-foot drop with lava to greet anyone foolish enough to fall off. Dead in the center of the platform is a large, cocoon-looking object. It is glowing brightly blue and emitting an extremely loud humming noise, so loud that it hurts the ears.

As they all step into the room, the blue light from the cocoon-looking object starts to shimmer and then turns into a dark red. It immediately bursts open to reveal Scarlet. Scarlet is floating in midair with his right leg arched up and his hair in a giant ponytail hanging off the back of his head. He lowers himself to the ground and turns around to Von.

"I'm so glad all of you could join me today," Scarlet says to everyone.

"Today will be your last!" Von says to Scarlet.

"Oh will it now?" Scarlet asks Von.

Scarlet sends a shockwave out at Von, but Pelisus puts up a protective barrier to block it.

"I'm impressed, old man. I didn't think you were that powerful," Scarlet says to Pelisus.

"I've got many tricks up my sleeve that you don't know about," Pelisus replies.

Scarlet laughs manically before saying, "Me too."

"Hyah!" Scarlet yells out loud, sending everyone but Von up against the walls of the room and binding them there.

"This fight is between me and you, little brother," Scarlet says to Von.

"I wouldn't have it any other way" Von says.

Scarlet summons a long bastard sword to his side and charges toward Von with his weapon drawn. Von charges toward scarlet as they clash blades. Von tries to swing at Scarlet from the right, but he is blocked by Scarlet's sword, so he throws in a head butt, knocking Scarlet a few feet back.

"You've gotten better I see, brother. This should be fun."

Scarlet aims his hand at the ground and sends a shockwave out toward Von. Von impales his weapons into the ground and uses them to balance himself as he does a front flip over the shockwave and brings both blades down onto Scarlet. Scarlet blocks Vons attack and laughs. He elbows Von in the face, causing his lip to bleed profusely. Von spits the blood in Scarlet's face and lunges in for an attack but is kicked to the ground.

"You're still no match for me brother," Scarlet says with a snicker.

"Oh yeah?" Von says to Scarlet before gripping his weapons tightly.

Von charges at Scarlet and clashes his two swords against Scarlet's giant blade. Each clash echoes throughout the cave.

"Bloodlust, Von! Use it, I know you can do it!" Lenya shouts out, distracting Von for a split second.

The cold iron of Scarlet's bastard sword cuts through Von's armor and leaves a small wound on his left arm. Von shrugs off the pain and continues at Scarlet, swinging wildly, trying to get a lucky hit in on him. Scarlet, though, is an all-around better fighter than Von, making it almost impossible for Von to get a lucky hit.

"What do I have to do to piss you off, brother?" Scarlet asks.

"Just you being alive pisses me off enough," Von adds.

Scarlet throws himself back away from Von and floats over to Lenya. He grabs her by the hair and holds the bastard sword up to her neck.

"DON'T YOU DARE TOUCH HER!" Von screams at the top of his lungs.

"Ahh, so that's your trigger. Love," Scarlet says with a manic chuckle at the end.

Scarlet pulls out a dagger and jams it deep into Lenya's chest. Von's eyes light up in anger after seeing this, and he charges toward Scarlet. Scarlet returns to the platform and battles Von more. Each swing from Von becomes faster and harder to block then the last.

"Ahhhhhhhhh! You son of a bitch!" Von screams at Scarlet before raising both of his weapons and bringing them down on Scarlet's sword, breaking it in two.

With Scarlet now disarmed, Von pushes both of his blades deep into his abdomen and runs him over to the edge to throw him down into the lava. Just as Von is about to throw Scarlet off, Scarlet grabs a hold of Von and pulls him down too, both of them plummeting down below into the lava.

Meanwhile, Pelisus uses his magic to free the three of them and teleport them to the center platform. With Scarlet now dead, the cave begins the shake and crumble. Large rocks start falling down all around them. Pelisus is faced with the decision of letting Lenya die from the knife wound or trying to find Von down by the lava pits. Using his better judgment, he grabs a hold of Lenya and Luna's hand and teleports them out of the cave.

He takes them to his last place of mediation at the very bottom of the mountain where they originally made camp the day before. With Lenya seriously injured, Pelisus pulls the knife out and casts a healing spell onto her. It won't immediately help the wound, but it will prevent infection and internal bleeding.

"We need to get her back to Genisus as soon as possible," Pelisus says to Luna.

"But what about Von?"

"I don't think he will be joining us," Pelisus replies

As Von and Scarlet were falling, Scarlet chuckled, "You finally did it brother. You controlled your bloodlust ..." At the sound of Scarlet's voice, Von shoved his weapons even deeper into his brother, causing blood to spew out of his mouth. Right before they hit the lava, a large red barrier appeared and caught them in limbo. Scarlet still has one last trick up his sleeve.

"Brother, I'm not going to make it out of here, but if you want to, I suggest you listen to what I have to say.

"Follow the red rings; they're safe to step on. Keep your balance. Don't lose it and you'll be fine."

Von nodded and listened to his brother.

# Chapter 8
# The Aftermath

Pelisus and Luna used one of the tents as a stretcher and carried Lenya all the way back to Genisus. The journey took a few days, and Lenya only became sicker and weaker as time passed by, but once they got to Genisus, they were all warmly welcomed back, even Pelisus in his true form as a dark elf. Lenya immediately got the treatment she needed in Genisus and was nursed back to health within a week. Aside from a clean bill of health, Lenya also got news that she was pregnant.

In the days after they fled, Mt. Fornal erupted and imploded upon itself—something no one could have survived. A large funeral was held for Von in Genisus; even the royal king showed up and saluted the coffin they buried.

Many days passed without anyone seeing or hearing from Von. No letters came; no one could even get near Mt. Fornal still because of all the lava everywhere. After three months passed, Lenya was visited by a hooded man. The closemouthed stranger didn't say a single word to Lenya but instead handed her both of Von's swords and walked away. In his honor, they made a play about the journey and the finale of how Von killed Scarlet, a plague to all of Drylor.

After the king's death Lenya was made princess of Drylor, and Luna and Pelisus were now headmasters of the magician's guild.

Five long years have passed since the day Scarlet was slain. Lenya's son is now almost five years old and named after his father, Von. Every year they do the anniversary play to commemorate what Von did for the world. They also erected a statue of Von in the front of Genisus as thanks for saving their great city.

Today is the anniversary of Scarlet's death. Lenya, Luna, and Pelisus are all watching from their royal seats above the crowd while the crowd circles around the front of the stage. The floors are packed; everyone loves the action and adventure of the play and the intensity of the final fight with Scarlet. As the play continues, everyone cheers for the person playing as Von, a young male in his mid-twenties with golden brown hair and blue eyes.

As the final scene plays, the whole crowd goes silent. The final scene is the hooded man walking up to Lenya and handing her a fake set of Von's weapons. The real ones Lenya keeps in her room sealed away in a case. It is the only memory she has of him besides her child who looks just like his daddy.

As the final scene commences, the hooded man approaches Lenya's character and hands her the swords. She gratefully accepts them and starts to cry, knowing well what it meant. As the hooded man walks away and toward the edge of the stage, he tears off his cloak and hood and turns around to face the crowd. The crowd gasps in awe at who the hooded man is.

"Is that … is that Von!" Lenya shouts.

"Lenya, my love, come to me!" Von screams down from the stage.

Lenya quickly leaves her seat and tears down the stairs of the castle out onto the stage. When she reaches Von, she throws her arms around him and gives him a big, long kiss. Both of them have tears rushing down their faces, as this is the first time they have seen each other in five long years. Luna bolts onto the stage and throws her arms around both Lenya and Von. Pelisus walks down and shakes Von's hand and gives him the nod, knowing he is happy to see Von again.

"Von, I have someone I would like you to meet," Lenya says to Von

"Come here, baby, meet your daddy."

Von sees the kid and drops to his knees. Tears fill his eyes as his heartbeat increases. The little kid is shy at first but runs over to Von and throws his arms around him, happy to finally meet his father. With Von holding his child in his arms, the crowd bursts into applause, giving him a standing ovation.